"Is something wrong?" she questioned, concern washing over her face.

"No," Guy replied as he suddenly slipped both his arms around her waist and torso and pulled her tightly to him.

The gesture knocked the wind from Dahlia's lungs as she felt her body melding easily against his. She clutched the front of Guy's T-shirt, her eyes lifted to his. His stare was intoxicating and Dahlia could feel herself slipping into the depths of his gaze, losing every ounce of her sensibilities in a wealth of longing. She suddenly felt as if a part of her soul was sliding home. The connection was so strong, so intense that she gasped loudly, the shock of the moment making it difficult for her to breathe.

Without giving it a second thought Dahlia wrapped her arms around Guy's neck. His mouth was only a fraction of an inch from hers, and in a swift, delicate motion Guy suddenly kissed her, capturing her mouth with determination as he pressed his closed lips against her closed lips. His touch was velvet, soft and gentle, the sweetest caress of skin against skin, and Dahlia instinctively knew that no other man could ever kiss her like that.

Books by Deborah Fletcher Mello

Harlequin Kimani Romance

In the Light of Love
Always Means Forever
To Love a Stallion
Tame a Wild Stallion
Lost in a Stallion's Arms
Promises to a Stallion
Seduced by a Stallion
Forever a Stallion
Passionate Premiere

DEBORAH FLETCHER MELLO

Writing since forever, Deborah Fletcher Mello can't imagine herself doing anything else. Her first romance novel, *Take Me To Heart,* earned her a 2004 Romance Slam Jam nomination for Best New Author. In 2005 she received Book of the Year and Favorite Heroine nominations for her novel *The Right Side of Love,* and in 2009 won an *RT Book Reviews* Reviewer's Choice Award for her ninth novel, *Tame a Wild Stallion.* Deborah's eleventh novel, *Promises to a Stallion,* earned her a 2011 Romance Slam Jam nomination for Hero of the Year.

For Deborah, writing is as necessary as breathing and she firmly believes that if she could not write she would cease to exist. For Deborah, the ultimate thrill is to weave a story that leaves her audience feeling full and complete, as if they've just enjoyed an incredible meal. Born and raised in Connecticut, Deborah now maintains base camp in North Carolina but considers home to be wherever the moment moves her.

Dear Reader,

Welcome to the Boudreaux family out of New Orleans! Much like my beloved Stallion family, I am just head over heels for the Boudreauxs. And I'm hoping you'll come to love them as much as I do.

The family is headed by parents Senior and Katherine Boudreaux and there are nine siblings in all: Mason, Maitlyn, Donovan, Katrina, Darryl, Kendrick, Kamaya, Guy and Tarah. What I love about this family is that they are just plain "folk," a family bonded by much love. Each has achieved varying levels of success and wealth in their lives. There's the business tycoon, the agent, the judge, the engineer, the entrepreneur, the free spirit, the actor and the student. What is constant between them all is that they are grounded in their faith and their love for God and family. With the Boudreaux there will be some drama, much drama and drama to the nth degree. And, of course, you can always expect a Stallion or two to drop by when you least expect. The doors are open for much to come and I can't begin to tell you how excited I am!

As always, I appreciate the love and support that you continue to show me. I love to hear what you think so please don't hesitate to contact me at DeborahMello@aol.com.

Until the next time, take care and God bless.

With much love,

Deborah Fletcher Mello

www.deborahmello.blogspot.com

Chapter 1

"Dahlia!"

"Here, Dahlia!"

"Dahlia, smile!"

Dahlia Morrow could not have been happier as she stepped out of the limousine in front of the Kodak Theatre on Hollywood Boulevard for the Eighty-Fifth Academy Awards. The paparazzi were desperate for her attention as cameras flashed around her and complete strangers screamed her name as if they were old friends.

"We love you, Dahlia!"

Dahlia stood in the requisite pose at the beginning of the red carpet, one hand perched pristinely against the curve of her hip. She smiled sweetly as her gaze skated over the landscape of actors and film critics, photographers and television hosts who were out in full force.

Being front and center was typical for the long list of film personalities present, but few filmmakers had ever received the kind of attention that Dahlia was receiving. Dahlia Morrow was an exception to the iconic rules; her fame had grown to significant proportions despite her best efforts to stay out of the limelight. From the start of her career to that very moment, the attention lavished on her had been formidable, as if she'd been the face in front of the cameras and not the brain trust behind them. And all because of her very brief romantic connection to one of the film industry's biggest stars; the majority of it had been headline fodder for the tabloids. Recognizing an opportunity, Dahlia had fostered the public's fascination with her into a highly recognized brand. Turning that moment of cause célèbre to her advantage now made her accomplishments instant news success.

Dahlia continued her slow stroll down the red carpet, pausing for snapshots and interviews. All of her hard work for the past two years had culminated in this one evening and she wanted to savor every moment of it. She paused in reflection, the moment captured for posterity as cameras continued to flash around her. Her brilliant smile dazzled her admirers.

Her first film project had been a two-minute short, a senior project in college. Her film teacher had submitted the assignment to a nationwide competition, and when Dahlia's had been selected best overall, winning her an internship with one of the largest film studios on the West Coast, her career in the movie industry was born.

And tonight her talent was being acknowledged by the industry with her latest film, *Victory's Daughter,* which was nominated for seven Academy Awards, including Best Picture and Best Director. Reviewers, pundits and bookies were predicting *Victory's Daughter* would sweep the Oscars, and Dahlia was betting on herself, as well.

This was her night, and Dahlia imagined that the only thing that could have made the moment more perfect was if she was walking the red carpet with a man she was head over heels in love with. Walking the red carpet with Drake Houston, however, would do. The renowned actor and playwright reveled in his own notoriety. Besides, he looked good with his windblown blond locks and ocean-blue eyes. Side by side they made a handsome couple. It would play nicely on the entertainment news and the cover of *Variety* magazine, Dahlia thought.

She beamed as one of the top radio personalities and television hosts rushed her with a microphone in his hand. In her classic Christian Dior couture gown and Christian Louboutin red-bottomed heels, she looked absolutely stunning. And her face radiated joy.

"Ryan, it's great to be here!" Dahlia exclaimed.

"Well, you look great," the host declared. "How does it feel to be the center of attention tonight?"

Dahlia smiled sweetly. "Well, I can tell you that I'm immensely proud that *Victory's Daughter* has gotten the many accolades it has. I loved the story, and I loved being able to tell it on film. I have to acknowledge the amazing cast and crew who helped to make it such a success. I couldn't have done it without them, and I'm confident that Brad, Hillary and Halle will all walk away with Oscars tonight for their stunning performances."

After fielding a few more questions, Dahlia continued to make her way down the red-carpeted path, posing for pictures and doing short interviews for the other major networks until she and Drake made their way to the building's entrance and were whisked inside and escorted to their seats.

Once inside she expressed her annoyance with her escort. "Drake, dear, you are going to wrinkle my dress with all the hugging. I need a little breathing room, my friend."

Drake chuckled warmly. "Can you blame me for wanting to hold tight to you, beautiful? You know how much I adore you, Dahlia!" He leaned to kiss her closed mouth but was met with her cheek instead.

The woman rolled her eyes, taking a deep inhale of breath. "Drake, you know I adore you and I consider you one of my closest friends, but you and I don't roll like that. And I hate having to say that over and over again. I don't want us to become bad friends, so please—" she paused momentarily "—please, cut me some slack!"

Drake heaved a deep sigh and nodded. "I had to try, Dahlia. What kind of man would I be if I didn't?" he asked with a slight shrug and a wry smile.

Dahlia chuckled softly, reaching up to give him a light kiss on his cheek. "I still love you, but you'll need to find someone else to take home to bed tonight."

Laughing, Drake gave her a quick wink. "You won't be disappointed if I do?"

She shook her head. "Not at all! But for now I need to go freshen up my makeup. Why don't you go say hello to Eastwood? He looks like he wants to speak with you," she said as she turned. She tossed him a quick look over her shoulder. "And don't worry if I don't come back. I'll make sure there's someone else here to take my place." She sauntered in the opposite direction.

"Take care of that for me!" Drake laughed as he blew her a kiss.

Out in the lobby, she gestured for one of the Academy pages. The young woman smiled excitedly at her. "Yes, Ms. Morrow? How may I help you?"

"I absolutely love my dress," Dahlia whispered as she leaned in conspiratorially. "But it's not the most comfortable thing to sit down in." She giggled softly. "Would you please send a seat-filler to my spot? I plan to stay in the greenroom until it's my turn to present."

"Yes, Ms. Morrow. Will Mr. Houston be joining you?"

Dahlia shook her head. "No, don't disturb him. He'll be fine. Just send someone very, very pretty to sit beside him," she said as she headed down the corridor toward the back of the stage, where there was a holding area for performers and those who were presenting.

As she rounded the corner, Dahlia ran smack into Owen Kestner, one of the evening's nominees for Best Supporting Actor. A former NFL professional, the rough-and-tumble linebacker smiled at her excitedly.

"Dahlia Morrow! Aren't you a sight for sore eyes!" the handsome man exclaimed.

"Owen, how are you?" Dahlia said sweetly.

"Just a little nervous. How about you?"

Dahlia nodded. "Nervous, too, but excited." She met his gaze evenly, taking note of his good looks and muscular frame. There was a mischievous gleam in his eyes as he stared at her intently. "So who's your date this evening?" she asked coyly.

The man chuckled warmly. "I'm riding solo tonight," he said, tossing her a quick wink. "But I saw you came with Drake Houston."

Dahlia smiled as she took a step closer to him. She drew her fingers against the front of his shirt, adjusting his bow tie and the front of his tuxedo jacket. She tilted her head to stare up at him. "I did come with Drake, but it doesn't mean I'll be leaving with him," she said, her tone dropping to a seductive whisper.

Owen smiled, his eyes brightening with interest. "And I imagine you'll be hitting all the A-list parties after the ceremony?"

Dahlia grinned. "If that works for you?" she said, sensing that her A-list access was all that he would be looking for.

"Would you mind if my friend Charles tagged along?" he queried, his eyes wide with anticipation.

Dahlia laughed. "Not at all."

Owen nodded eagerly, his smile bright. "My limo or yours?"

Dahlia laughed, winking her own eye. "Yours. I don't want to leave my friend Drake stranded."

* * *

"But it's not like you had tickets?" Mason Boudreaux said, eyeing his younger brother with confusion. "Or did you have tickets?"

Guy Boudreaux cut his eyes skyward, annoyed by his older brother's question. He nodded his head, the long length of his dreadlocks waving against his broad shoulders. "Of course I had tickets. Good seats, as a matter of fact. And invitations to the best Oscar parties. You can't beat that kind of networking, brother!"

Mason nodded his understanding. "Well, I appreciate you giving up the Oscars to make it to my wedding."

"What are best men for?" Guy said, beaming widely as he looked from his brother to his new sister-in-law.

The newly minted Phaedra Boudreaux smiled back. "So, what will you do when you do get back to California?" she asked, snuggling close to her new husband.

"I'll be filming a commercial next week. I'm now the spokesman for the new Chanel for Men cologne."

Having a lightbulb moment, Guy suddenly leaned forward in his seat. "Hey, by the way, Phaedra, I could really use some new head shots. Do you think you can hook me up?"

Mason rolled his eyes. "That means he wants a family discount!" he said as he hugged Phaedra tightly.

"No," Guy protested. "That means I want it free."

Phaedra, an award-winning professional photographer, laughed. "I think we could probably work something out."

Guy winked. "I'd like that," he said, laughing easily, his magnetic smile beaming brightly.

Mason shook his head. After a lengthy holiday abroad he was ready to be off a plane and back on land. He'd needed to resolve some unfinished business in Thailand, and the past week had been a test of his fortitude. He was thankful to finally be back in the United States and headed home.

After whirlwind visits to Asia and France, he and his family had stopped in London to refuel and again in New Orleans to drop off his sister Kamaya and her twin, Kendrick, at their parents' home. Now they were headed to Dallas, Texas, to spend time with the Stallion family, Phaedra's newfound kin, four brothers who shared her bloodline. Guy would be continuing on to Los Angeles by his lonesome. And Guy was anxious to get back.

"My money's on *Victory's Daughter* to win Best Picture," Guy was saying. He and Phaedra were knee-deep in a conversation about movies.

"I absolutely loved *Victory's Daughter,*" Phaedra exclaimed. "And it has to get an award for Best Cinematography. The imagery was spectacular!"

"Have you ever thought about doing films?" Guy asked, remembering that his new sister-in-law was renowned for her skills as a photojournalist.

Phaedra shook her head. "Not really. I love still photography. I can't imagine myself doing anything else."

"I understand that," Guy said. "That's how I feel about acting."

"So, who else do you think will win tonight?" Mason interjected.

Guy paused for a minute. "I'm betting on Dahlia

Morrow for Best Director, and Halle stole the show with her performance as Victory, so she's my bet for Best Actress."

"Do you know Dahlia?" Phaedra queried.

Guy shook his head. "No, but I've been looking for an opportunity to meet her. I would love to be in one of her films."

Phaedra smiled. "Well, I'd love to introduce you two. Dahlia and I are sorority sisters. We've been good friends for years," she noted casually.

Guy nodded excitedly, gesturing with two thumbs pointed skyward. "That's what I'm talkin' about, another hookup! I am truly loving you, sister-in-law."

Chapter 2

Leslie Stanton met Dahlia at the front door of her office with a large caffe latte and the morning paper. The robust black woman was shaking her head as Dahlia crossed the room to her upholstered chair and took a seat.

"Pray tell, how did you manage to have two dates for the Oscars?"

Dahlia shrugged. "Congratulations to you, too," she said, meeting the woman's gaze.

Leslie laughed. "Congratulations! It was an Oscar landslide! You don't see that every year."

Dahlia laughed with her. "Next time we're sweeping Visual Effects and Best Original Screenplay, too. Mark my words!" she said as she opened the paper to the front page and stared.

The headline read "Oscar's Golden Girl" and featured three images: Dahlia standing alone page center, a shot of her and Drake Houston to the left and another of her and Owen Kestner to the right. The tabloids were having a field day thinking she had left Drake standing at the Academy door while she'd partied the night away with Owen. She shook her head as she took a sip of her morning drink.

"Did you sleep with him?" Leslie asked, dropping into the seat in front of the large desk.

"Him who?"

"Whichever man you left with," Leslie said with a raised eyebrow.

"I left with Owen, but he went home with his good friend Charles," Dahlia said, peering over the top of her coffee cup. "His *very* good friend," she emphasized, hinting at the relationship that had already been gossiped about in hushed whispers.

Wide-eyed, Leslie shook her head and chuckled. "Hush yo' mouth!"

"So did you sleep with the other one?" Leslie continued.

"I never sleep with *any* of them. That's why I have such a problem when I want to get rid of them. Most men think if they can't bed you on their timetable, then your virtue is something they suddenly need to conquer."

Her friend laughed. "Since you mentioned it, Drake called for you," she said. "Something about doing dinner this week if you're available."

"See!" Dahlia exclaimed. "They just won't go away."

Leslie laughed as she tossed a stack of folders onto Dahlia's desk. "You have back-to-back appointments starting at eleven o'clock. First, there's a conference call with the casting agency, then lunch with the Bresdan Arts Foundation to discuss financing and then the interview with Oprah and her people. From there you have a photo shoot for *People* magazine, an hour with your personal trainer and then dinner with the studio execs," Leslie concluded as she tapped one last notation into Dahlia's smartphone.

She passed the device to her friend. "Your alarms are all set on vibrate. Stay on schedule and you should be done for the day by nine but by latest ten o'clock tonight. And don't forget to call your aunt Minnie and wish her a happy birthday."

Dahlia chuckled softly. "See, when would I actually have time to sleep with a man if you didn't put it on my schedule?"

"So, I need to schedule some quality alone time with Drake so you can get you some?"

"Uh, no!"

"Owen?"

"Uh, double no!"

Leslie laughed with her. "Well, we need to schedule something and soon because you can't keep tossing these boys away like you do your shoes."

"I never toss my shoes away. I love my shoes."

"But you only wear them three, maybe four times. I can't remember the last time a man lasted that long with you."

"My shoes don't get in my way. A man usually will."

"Well, every woman needs herself a DOC," Leslie said, her eyebrows lifted, her expression humorous. "We need to find you one, maybe even two."

Dahlia looked momentarily confused. "What is a DOC?" she questioned, her own eyebrows raised in query.

Leslie laughed. "DOC…dick-on-command!" she said.

The two women giggled until tears were raining from their eyes.

Leslie gestured for her to get a move on it. "There is a car downstairs waiting for you. The driver has your itinerary and will be at your beck and call until he drops you at your front door tonight. Take the conference call on your way to the restaurant."

Dahlia blew out a deep sigh as she headed in the direction of the door. Leslie called her name just as her hand reached for the knob.

"Yes?"

"I'm really proud of you, Dahlia. You really done good, girl!"

Dahlia met her friend's bright smile with one of her own. "*We* done good, girl! 'Cause I couldn't have done any of it without you."

Disconnecting the conference call, Dahlia took a quick moment to close her eyes and reflect. The limousine was stuck tire-deep in a line of midday traffic, crawling at a snail's pace toward her afternoon appointment. Her day was just getting started and already she was wishing that it could be over. But a breather wasn't going to propel her career skyward. Only hard work would make this year's awards program seem like practice for what she hoped to accomplish in the next few years.

Making movies wasn't easy, and Dahlia predicted that because of her sentimental connection to the project, making her next movie would prove to be the biggest challenge of her career. With most of the pre-production tasks already in the works, she still had a lengthy list of things that needed to be accomplished.

The script for her next project was all her, written the year she'd graduated from film school. She'd been fine-tuning it ever since, determined to create a work of sheer perfection if such a thing were possible. With her award-winning night, she wanted to ensure that the studios would be well on board, and she had her fingers crossed that her scheduled dinner with the executives would be their green light on the project.

If the studio approved, financing was a given. But Dahlia already had a plan B in place, just in case, knowing that in the film industry nothing was ever as easy as it seemed. And with a multimillion-dollar budget at risk, Dahlia was determined to make the film work. The director was a given, as well, because no one but Dahlia was going to control this film's artistic and dramatic aspects.

Now they were casting, and confirmation had come that Golden Globe winner Zahara Ginolfi has signed on for the lead female role. Dahlia smiled, nodding her head ever so slightly. Once she found the perfect male lead, the rest would be easy as pie. The casting director already had a prospect in mind, a man Dahlia was scheduled to meet the following week.

Dahlia knew that finding the perfect locations, budgeting and signing on the production team and crew, in addition to a host of other chores, were already in the works and would fall into place when she needed them to. She had faith and a fire in the pit of her stomach to make it happen no matter what sacrifices she might have to make. And Dahlia was used to making sacrifices—the greatest forfeitures occurred in her personal life.

There was no time for a relationship with anyone who was anxious for her attention. So Dahlia refused to allow herself to get close to any man who might be a distraction or demanding of her time. And despite what people thought—the tabloids had dubbed her the "love 'em and leave 'em wildflower"—she didn't have herself a DOC, no man that she kept around for convenience or otherwise. Folks didn't even begin to have a clue about Dahlia's love life. Because Dahlia had yet to find love, and when she did, she couldn't imagine herself being so casual about it.

The driver pulled the car in front of Osteria Mozza Restaurant. Opening her eyes, Dahlia took a deep breath of air. Taking a quick glance into her compact mirror, she dabbed at her nose with the powder puff. With her game face on she headed inside, ready to talk a few thousand dimes out of a few thousand rocks.

Chapter 3

Guy took one last lap around the enclosed track. Dwight Brooks, his personal trainer, waited with a stopwatch at the finish line. Dwight had spent the past three hours putting him through his paces, and Guy was past ready to be done.

Guy came to an abrupt stop in front of his friend, bending forward at the waist, his palms pressed against his upper thighs as he fought to catch his breath. Dwight slapped him heartily on his back.

"Nice! That was one of your best times," he said, jotting notes into a small notebook he'd pulled from his back pocket.

Guy nodded, inhaling deeply. He stood upright, his hands moving to the line of his hips. "Thanks, but it feels like you have me training for a marathon and not a movie."

"Same difference," Dwight answered with a shrug of his shoulders.

Guy chuckled. "I hear you," he said as the two moved in the direction of the locker room.

"So, what time is your audition?" Dwight asked, eyeing the watch on his wrist.

"Soon. I have just enough time to shower and change."

"This one's big, huh?"

"Big enough," Guy said as he unlocked the metal enclosure that housed his personal possessions. "I'm auditioning for Dahlia Morrow," he pronounced, lifting his gym bag from inside the locker.

"Sweet!"

"Yes, I hear she is," Guy said, a smirk pulling at his full lips.

Dwight laughed. "And I presume the part is, as well?"

Guy laughed with him. "It's a great role, actually. I loved the script," he said. "I'm thinking it's destiny, too, because I was just telling my family that I wanted to meet her. Apparently, she and my sister-in-law are old friends. So, I'm thinking it's fate in action that I mention her name and now I'm auditioning for her."

"I'm sure it is," Dwight agreed. He extended a closed hand in Guy's direction, and the two men bumped fists. "I've got to run. Good luck with your audition," he said. With a slight wink of his eye, he added, "And the woman. I will see you tomorrow, same time."

"Sounds like a plan," Guy responded as he headed in the direction of the showers. "But go easy on a brother next time."

"Yeah, like that's going to happen. I have a reputation to maintain, too, you know!"

Guy waved goodbye, chuckling heartily as he watched his friend exit the gym.

Stripping out of his sports clothes, Guy stepped into a warm shower, allowing the spray of water to cascade over his face and down his broad chest. As he lathered his deep caramel–complexioned skin with a spice-scented body wash, the thick suds painted his naked form with a luxurious froth. His muscles had finally begun to relax beneath the rise of the warm mist, and he savored the sensations, stretching the tightness out of each sinew.

He heaved a deep sigh. He had only been half kidding when he'd said that fate was directing his footsteps. His agent's early morning call had come as a complete surprise. Both of them had been stunned that the casting agent for Dahlia Morrow's next film had requested he meet with the lady herself without asking him for a screen test.

Despite his own A-list status in the industry and a long list of blockbuster movies under his belt, he was still occasionally made to jump through hoops for leading men roles in movies that he didn't actively pursue or have a hand in producing. And despite the many leading men roles out there, the selection for black males was still a bit slim. But filmmakers like Dahlia Morrow were attempting to change the dynamics, and some sort of cosmic fate was bringing the two of them together.

Stepping out of the shower, he reached for an over-size white towel, swiping at the dampness against his skin. Thirty minutes later he was dressed and headed out to meet providence, hopeful that Dahlia Morrow, and kismet, were about to grace him with favor.

Although it had already been a very long day, Dahlia couldn't help feeling like the rest of it was going to be well worth her efforts. But as she disconnected her cell phone, turning the ringer to vibrate, she couldn't hide the frustration that painted her expression. Finding funding for her movie was proving to be the bane of her existence; the studios had been a huge disappointment to her. Despite its accolades and having grossed over fifty million dollars in box office receipts, *Victory's Daughter* was still considered "underperforming" by industry standards, and that fact had potential investors for her next film all too ready to tell her no.

But the box office wasn't a true measure of the film's worth. Nor did it speak to the film as art or the merit of her next venture. So telling Dahlia no only served to make her want to prove them all wrong, moving her to consider investing her own money into the project. A prospect her attorneys, financial advisers and friends were adamantly against.

Doing what she loved shouldn't be so hard, she mused. But Hollywood was ruled by a patriarchy with black women existing only along the sidelines of the industry. Although perceived as a liberal, diverse space

that welcomed creativity and difference, the film industry was still overwhelmingly white and male—a good
ol' boys club in full control. It made it difficult at best
for Dahlia to do what she loved.

Despite women making films for more than one
hundred years, Kathryn Bigelow had been the first
woman to win an Academy Award for directing, taking home the prize. Dahlia was the first woman of color
to claim the honor and, at the age of twenty-eight, also
the youngest filmmaker, male or female, to be hon-
ored. But women filmmakers of any race or age had
yet to experience the same levels of success as their
male counterparts, and Dahlia was intent on changing that. Wanting more than anything to just tell good
stories, she had to be diligent and persistent and, like
every black woman who was making films, she had
to be resilient.

Dahlia took a sip of her bottled springwater, tapping heavily against the tabletop with the pen that
rested between her fingers. She glanced down at the
diamond-encrusted watch that adorned her slim wrist.
She'd arrived early for her casting, and she still had a
few minutes before the actor she was meeting was due
to arrive.

The casting agency had scheduled this appointment.
If she'd been able, Dahlia would have canceled without giving it a second thought. But she needed to stay
on schedule, and staying on schedule meant finding a
male lead and locking him into contract as quickly as
possible. So canceling hadn't been a real option for her.

Dahlia looked down at the IMDB résumé the casting agency had faxed over to her. She was meeting one of Hollywood's golden boys, the infamous Guy Boudreaux. His professional résumé was a plethora of some very big box office successes; his recent portrayal of the new James Bond authenticated a career that would surely go down in the history books. Having spent the past evening watching two of his independent films, Dahlia could not deny the man's talent. His ability to capture the essence of his characters and breathe life into them surpassed his youthful twenty-eight years and made him exactly what Dahlia was looking for in her male lead.

A commotion at the restaurant's entrance drew her attention. She looked up to see Guy Boudreaux as he was accosted by an eager female fan. He stopped to sign an autograph, and there was no missing his welcoming demeanor as he posed for a picture with a family of five, chatting with the group as if they were old friends.

Dahlia's eyes widened with interest. Guy Boudreaux was imposing in stature, standing just over six feet tall. Dressed in a black silk suit and white dress shirt opened at the collar, he was quite the male specimen. His chest was broad, flanked by wide shoulders. His legs were long, and the slacks he wore nicely complemented the hard, full curves of a very high backside. His complexion was dark caramel with the faintest undertone of buttercream, warm and delectable as it stretched taut over clearly defined muscles. A crown of black dreadlocks hung past his shoulders, and just a hint of facial hair, the beginnings of a neatly trimmed mustache and goatee, complemented his chiseled facial features. He was a Greek Adonis with an artistic aura, his look a nice blend of bohemian flair and classic styling. It was clear that he wore his confidence like a neon blanket draped over his torso, bright and abundant. The man was handsome beyond words, and Dahlia felt her breath catch in her throat as he crossed the room in her direction.

"Ms. Morrow, Guy Boudreaux," he said as he extended a large hand in greeting. "It's a pleasure to meet you."

Dahlia lifted her gaze to meet his, feeling overwhelmingly starstruck as words failed her. She nodded as he clasped her hand beneath his, shaking it firmly. His palm was silky smooth as it glided over hers like a sensual kiss.

"May I sit down?" Guy asked, amusement crossing his expression, her hand still trapped beneath his.

Dahlia took a deep breath as she nodded her head, slowly pulling her hand from his. Her fingers tingled, the sensation sweeping like wildfire through her body. It was intense and disturbing, and she tried to stall the feelings by clasping both of her hands together in her lap. "Excuse me," she said, clearing her throat. "Of course, have a seat, Mr. Boudreaux."

She eyed him keenly as he slid into the leather-covered booth beside her.

"Please, call me Guy. I hope I'm not late," he said, his gaze still locked with hers, a brilliant smile of pearl-white teeth beaming at her.

She shook her head, desperate to clear the cloud that had mysteriously consumed her. "No, you're right on time actually," she finally answered. "And it's definitely a pleasure to meet you. Your reputation has preceded you."

"Yours, as well," Guy said with a light chuckle. "Congratulations on your recent victory."

Dahlia smiled sweetly. "Thank you. I hope you know that I'm looking to do that again with this new project."

Guy gestured ever so slightly with his head, a warm smile filling his face. "I'm thinking that won't be a problem. It's a great story, the script is on point and with me as the lead character, it can't help but be a success," he said teasingly.

Dahlia chuckled warmly. "So, tell me what you really think," she said.

"Seriously, this project has great potential, and I think I'd be a wonderful asset to your vision. But if I can ask you one question?"

"Of course."

"Tell me more about the story. When I read it I got the sense that there was some background history there that wasn't being told."

Dahlia smiled, her eyes locking with his. She nodded her head slowly, her thoughts drifting ever so briefly. Guy was right, and his intuition gave her reason to pause.

"There is history there. My history. The lead characters are modeled after my grandparents. They met in 1935 when my grandmother was barely fourteen and my grandfather was sixteen. They were inseparable from that moment on. Both of their parents had forbidden them to be together and they were defiant, doing exactly what they wanted instead. And when Granny became pregnant at a young age, it set off a chain of events that neither of them were really prepared for."

"And they really did meet in a dance hall?"

Dahlia nodded her head. "My grandmother was an extraordinary dancer. She loved the music and being out on a dance floor. And my grandfather loved her and whatever it was that she loved."

"Your grandparents, are they still living?"

She took a deep breath, a hint of tears misting her eyes. "No. He passed on when I was just a little girl, and my grandmother died last year. She was ninety-one."

"I'm so sorry."

Dahlia shrugged her shoulders as she took another deep breath. The memory of losing her beloved grandmother still haunted her. The woman's passing had been expected; the family had sat vigil for almost a week in one of the best hospice facilities in the city. But even the knowing hadn't been able to minimize the tremendous hurt that had completely devastated Dahlia when the moment had come.

There was no missing the emotion that passed over Dahlia's face. Guy found himself taken aback by her expression. The pain of it felt like a needle prick through his heart, and in that moment he would have done anything to take the hurt from her eyes and make everything well again. He resisted the temptation to reach out and touch her, to strum his fingers against the back of her hand and down the length of her arm.

As if reading his thoughts, Dahlia pulled her hands back into her lap. She met his gaze, and his stare was like a soothing balm. Guy smiled. The warmth of it seared through her like a bolt of lightning. She gasped lightly.

Clearing her throat, she finally said, "I am still fine-tuning the script. I've also felt like there was something that was missing in the story line, something I haven't been able to define yet."

Dahlia then tossed him a smile of her own. "What I can tell you is that when they met, my grandmother had snuck out of the house to see Nat King Cole. He was performing at that dance hall. He was in his teens himself, his own career just beginning."

"Nat King Cole! Amazing!"

"Granny thought so, too. She was enamored with the man and always said that Nat would be her second husband if my granddaddy didn't act right."

Guy chuckled softly. "Good to know. 'When I Fall in Love' and 'Dream a Little Dream of Me' were two of my favorites of his."

Dahlia's smile widened, pleasantly surprised that he was even familiar with the late crooner's bibliography.

Taking note of the astonished look in her eyes, Guy laughed heartily. "I am an old soul," he said matter-of-factly.

"Interesting." Dahlia leaned forward in her seat, her elbows coming to rest on the table as she clasped her hands beneath her chin. She sat in quiet deliberation for a brief moment before continuing, "I'll be honest with you, Guy, it's looking like the studios are not going to back this project. Not as I had hoped they would. It seems that I will be producing this film independently, on a significantly lower budget, but I intend for it to rival any mainstream film production out there."

"So, what you're telling me is that I won't be making a million plus for this role?"

"Not even close. Still interested?"

Guy met her gaze and held it, intently studying the delicate lines of her features. Dahlia Morrow was a stunning woman. Even more beautiful than the magazine images of her that he'd seen. She had beautiful eyes, dark seductive orbs that a man could lose himself in if he were so inclined. Her full lips parted ever so slightly, her tongue snaking past to quickly lick the line of her mouth. When she did he felt an unexpected surge of heat through his groin. He suddenly reached for her bottle of water and took a deep swig.

Eyebrows lifted, Dahlia laughed at his forwardness. "We can order you your own drink if you want," she said, still giggling softly as she snatched her water bottle from his hands.

Guy grinned sheepishly. "Umm…that's umm…not necessary," he muttered. "You looked like you didn't mind sharing." His expression was teasing as his eyes locked with hers for the umpteenth time.

There was a pause as they sat staring at each other, both grinning widely.

"You're funny," Dahlia said, finally breaking the silence.

"Not as funny as you are, Ms. Morrow!"

Dahlia rolled her eyes.

"On a serious note," Dahlia said, deliberately changing the subject, "this movie is proving to be more of a challenge than I anticipated."

"You're a beautiful, black woman trying to move a mountain, Dahlia. No one said that would be easy."

"No, they didn't. Nor did they say my wanting to move that mountain means you or any other man has to be there pushing with me."

Guy smiled. It was an easy lift to his mouth that warmed Dahlia's spirit. "What kind of a man would I be if I wasn't willing to give a woman who is so determined a helping hand?"

Dahlia considered his question before responding. "Not the man I would want starring in my next movie," she said as she extended a manicured hand in his direction. Dahlia didn't miss his holding tight to her fingers a second longer than necessary, nor did she miss the heat that seemed to rise out of nowhere and radiate between them. She pulled her hand away, fighting not to show that she was uncomfortable with the sensations sweeping over her, vulnerability painting her expression.

Grateful for the alarm, she stole a quick glance at her smartphone as it vibrated against the tabletop. "I look forward to working with you, Mr. Boudreaux," she said as she stood up, moving to leave. "I will give your agent a call and make a formal offer. Welcome to my movie."

"The pleasure will be mine, Ms. Morrow," he said as he came to his feet. He tossed her a quick wink of his eye. "And thanks for the water."

Dahlia laughed warmly. "Don't thank me yet, Guy!" she said as she made her exit.

Guy stared intently after Dahlia as she eased her way out of the room. His eyes were not the only ones to follow after her, and he had to appreciate the view along with her other admirers. Dahlia Morrow was captivatingly beautiful.

Guy smiled widely, his gaze skating the lines of her formfitting dress. The red silk garment she wore was like wet paint slathered over the curves of her full bustline, thin waist and lush derriere. The woman had curves, a Rubenesque figure, all the stuff that could make a strong man beg on his knees for her attention.

As the waiter paused at the table, depositing the unpaid tab for that one bottle of water, Guy had to laugh, completely intrigued by Dahlia. As he deposited a twenty-dollar bill onto the table, he hated to admit that begging on his knees had surely crossed his mind, if only for a very brief moment.

Chapter 4

Leslie shook her head as she stood with Dahlia's requisite morning beverage in hand. Dahlia eyed her warily as she took hold of the cup and took the first sip of her drink.

"What?" Dahlia questioned, her eyes wide with curiosity. "What now?"

"You tell me," Leslie said, blocking Dahlia's path into her office.

"I don't have a clue what you're referring to," Dahlia said, her curiosity peaked.

Leslie smirked, meeting Dahlia's intense gaze. "Guy Boudreaux has been waiting for you. He's in your office."

Dahlia stood like stone, her mouth falling open in surprise. "Guy Boudreaux?"

Leslie nodded as she pointed to the closed office door. "And the casting agency delivered copies of his contract this morning. You didn't tell me that Guy Boudreaux had said yes," she whispered in a hushed breath.

"Must have slipped my mind," Dahlia whispered nonchalantly back. She took another sip of her drink, avoiding the look her dear friend was giving her.

"Do you remember when Idris agreed to do your short film? You called me before the ink was dry on the paper."

"I did."

"And when Brad came on board for *Victory* you sent me a text message as the man was signing."

"And your point?" Dahlia queried.

"You have a meeting with the black James Bond, the man agrees to be in your film and I only find out after the contracts are delivered *and* I find out from Guy and the delivery guy. That doesn't sound out of the norm to you?"

Dahlia shrugged as a wide grin filled her face. "Okay, so maybe it's a little unusual."

"I wonder why," Leslie said as she lifted a cashier's check from the pile of folders in her hand and passed it to Dahlia. "He was just about to leave, and I was supposed to give this to you."

Dahlia looked from the check to Leslie and back, her mouth dropping open in surprise. The six-figure amount was significant, and the accompanying note threw the woman completely off guard. Dahlia read it once, then a second and third time.

Leslie snatched the note from Dahlia's hands. She read out loud, still whispering, "'I look forward to doing business with you. We'll negotiate my executive producer responsibilities over our next bottle. Your turn to buy this time. Guy Boudreaux.'"

Dahlia shook her head as she moved in the direction of the door.

Leslie stalled her one last time. "And Phaedra called. She and her new husband heard good things about your movie and they are also interested in investing."

Dahlia shook her head. "Phaedra has a new husband?" she asked as her hand reached for the doorknob.

Her friend nodded. "A very wealthy husband. And her new hubby has very wealthy brothers, but then you already know that, right?"

A look of confusion crossed Dahlia's face. "I do?"

Leslie laughed. "Uh, yeah! It seems she and your new executive producer are related by marriage."

Dahlia's eyes widened considerably. "Phaedra married Guy's brother? Why weren't we invited to the wedding? Were we invited to the wedding?"

Leslie laughed again.

"Apparently, it was a quiet ceremony with just the two of them and their immediate families. Call her. Our sorority sister has a lot to catch you up on. And when you're done with your new friend in there, I want to hear every detail about your meeting with Guy Boudreaux and that bottle you two shared. Can't believe you didn't tell me you spent time with that fine man," Leslie fussed as Dahlia shook her head.

Studying the generous check one more time, Dahlia

wasn't sure whether she should throw her arms around the man's neck and hug him or squeeze the life out of him. Taking a deep breath, she opened the door to her office and stepped inside.

Guy Boudreaux sat in the leather executive's chair behind her glass-and-metal desk. His long legs were stretched out in front of him, his leather loafers resting on the desk's corner. His cell phone was tucked between his ear and shoulder as he chatted easily with someone on the other end, all the while flipping through the papers that had been on her desk.

As Dahlia closed the office door behind her, Guy greeted her with a wide grin and a slight wave of his hand. He seemed quite comfortable. *Too comfortable,* Dahlia thought. *And damn, if he didn't look good, too!* Walking to where he sat, Dahlia snatched her files from his hands, a look of annoyance on her face. He continued to grin at her as she pulled his phone away and disconnected his call. She dropped the device into his lap, then gave him a not-so-gentle push to move out of her seat.

"Executive producer? Isn't that a stretch?" she questioned.

Guy stood up, the length of his frame tall above her, and she was awed by the nearness of him. The man radiated body heat like an overworked furnace on a cold night. The heat was consuming, and she suddenly wanted to strip naked for relief. The sensations sweeping through her were unnerving. She took two steps back from him, fighting not to blatantly fan herself.

Guy laughed. "Well, hello to you, too, Dahlia."

"Guy." Dahlia eased her way around him to sit in her seat.

As she passed, her shoulder brushed against his arm, and the connection was like an igniting flame. Guy felt his body tense; the scent of her perfume threw lighter fluid on his rising emotions. Every muscle hardened beneath his skin. Dahlia gestured toward the empty chair, wishing for some distance between them.

Moving to the other side of the table and the cushioned chair in front of her desk, Guy sat down. He took a deep breath before he spoke, willing the tension away. "No, I don't think it's a stretch at all. In fact, I'm thinking it's quite appropriate in light of my very generous contribution."

Dahlia paused, fighting to focus her eyes on anything except his face. "I'm willing to concede that. As long as you understand it's strictly honorary." She crossed her arms over her chest, finally lifting her gaze to his.

Guy held her stare for a moment, startled by the intensity that pierced past her forest-thick lashes. The look she was giving him was intoxicating, and something like desire washed over him. He could only begin to imagine what she saw in his own eyes since desire was exactly what he was feeling for her. He crossed one leg over the other, hoping to hide the sudden rise of nature between them. He cleared his throat. "What? You mean you don't want me to be hands-on?"

"Truthfully, I want you to be exceptionally hands-*off*," Dahlia emphasized. "You get a script, you memorize and deliver your lines like the professional I know you are and it'll be all good between us."

"We'll see about that," he said lightly as he shifted the conversation, leaning forward in his seat. "What time are you buying me dinner tonight?"

"Why didn't you tell me you know my friend Phaedra?"

"Do you always answer a question by changing the subject with another question?" Guy countered.

Dahlia shrugged, feigning disinterest. "I'm not buying you dinner. If anything, I'll buy you a bottle of water, but that's about it. I don't mix business with pleasure, Mr. Boudreaux."

Guy nodded. "I'm glad to hear that," he responded, feigning his own disinterest, "because my intent is strictly business. I do, however, try to eat three square meals per day. And since I'm on a strict regimen, there's little that's pleasurable about it, not even the prospect of your company. So, I should be done by seven o'clock. Shall we meet at eight?"

Dahlia paused, the man's arrogance taking her by surprise. There was a hint of teasing in his tone, and that annoyed her, as well. For a brief moment she thought about throwing him out on his very delectable behind, but she refused to give him the satisfaction of knowing that he'd riled her.

"Tonight won't work. I have another commitment," she said finally.

"A date?" Guy asked curiously.

She ignored his query, amused that he would even think that he could question her plans. "I'll meet you tomorrow afternoon at Roscoe's," she responded. "Can you do three o'clock?"

Guy laughed. "Two would be better, so let's split the difference. Will two-thirty work for you?"

"Two-thirty it is," Dahlia said.

"Enjoy your date tonight, Dahlia," Guy said, tossing her a quick wink of his eye. He stood up and made his way to the door. He stopped short, turning back around to face her. "Oh, and to answer your other question, Phaedra married my older brother, Mason. She and I are family." His grin widened. "See you tomorrow, beautiful." He made his exit, his expression eager at the prospect.

Without responding, Dahlia leaned back in her seat. Leslie drew her attention as she cleared her throat in the doorway. The two friends locked gazes.

"And you won't do dinner why?" Leslie asked.

"Were you eavesdropping?"

"You know I was."

Dahlia shook her head. "Because he expected that I would just jump at the opportunity, and I'm not giving him that satisfaction."

Leslie laughed. "And lunch tomorrow will be your comeuppance?"

Dahlia smiled. "It's not dinner and he's not dictating the where and the when."

Leslie's eyes widened. "You like that man."

Dahlia's face scrunched up in annoyance, her eyes narrowing to thin slits. "He's an employee."

Leslie laughed again as she reached for Dahlia's smartphone and accessed the calendar on the device. She quickly tapped an entry into the database before passing the gadget back to the other woman.

"Something I don't know about?" Dahlia questioned, scanning the month's activity page.

Shrugging her shoulders, Leslie exited the room, still giggling softly.

Dahlia couldn't miss the appointments Leslie had noted for the following night and each day thereafter. The woman had scheduled hours of quality time for her and Guy Morrow, each notation followed by a string of hearts.

"Not funny!" Dahlia shouted. She had to laugh at her friend, shaking her head. But as she sat staring at the notation she couldn't help but imagine the possibilities, because Guy Boudreaux definitely had her imagination running rampant.

Dahlia couldn't remember the last time any man had taken her breath away, and meeting Guy had done just that. Everything about the delectable man had put her on sensory overload and ignited a fire through every nerve ending in her body. Guy Boudreaux had been a refreshing departure from the usual characters she'd come to know in Hollywood. His down-to-earth persona overshadowed the bad-boy, playboy image he often portrayed. The man had been funny, intuitive and too damn sexy for words. In fact, Dahlia mused, blowing out a deep sigh, Guy Boudreaux had been too much man for her to even begin to fathom, and she was giving every ounce of him much consideration.

"So, who's the doll you've checked Google for a million times on your laptop?" Darryl Boudreaux asked as he scanned the screen of his older brother's computer.

"What?"

"Dahlia Morrow. You've been spending a lot of time researching the woman. Is she an actress or something?"

Guy shook his head, reaching to close the lid of his laptop from his brother's prying eyes.

"Hey, I was optimizing your hard drive!" Darryl intoned.

"No, you were being nosy."

"I was doing that, too. She's cute, though. The woman has a body and then some."

Guy rolled his eyes at his brother's comment. "She's a filmmaker, one of the best. Do you follow the industry at all, Darryl?"

Darryl shrugged his broad shoulders. "I don't even own a television, why would I follow the film industry?"

"Uh, maybe to support your big brother?"

"I can support you without denigrating my mind with the garbage they're airing on TV these days. And I think I support you just fine. I installed your security system. I fixed your garbage disposal last week. I designed a new rooftop garden for you—construction starts in two days, by the way—and if you leave me alone, I can make sure you have the best access to the internet to keep scoping out your woman," Darryl said as he lifted the computer's top and resumed his search of Guy's database.

Guy laughed. "I wasn't scoping her out!"

Darryl cut his eyes toward his brother, indicating

that he knew better and wasn't buying his brother's protests.

"You need to worry about your own love life," Guy said, gesturing toward his brother's cell phone, which was vibrating against the desktop. "What's that, the hundredth time she's called?"

Darryl scowled, annoyance painting his features. He'd been ignoring the device for over an hour as his soon-to-be-ex girlfriend blew up his cell phone. He shook his head. "I told Asia that it wasn't working out and we needed to sit down and have a serious talk."

"I'm sure that's going to go well. I told you that girl was crazy from the start."

Darryl shrugged again, turning back to his task. "By the way, Maitlyn said to call her. She has some questions about you and your new woman, too."

"What did you say to her?"

"I didn't say anything to her. You hire your sister to be your manager and you don't think she's not going to know everything that's going on with you? Big brother, please. You even taught me better than that," Darryl said with a wry laugh. "And I'd bet my last dollar that if Maitlyn suspects something, then Mommy and the rest of the girls already know."

Guy headed to the bedroom of his penthouse apartment. He hated when his siblings peeped his hold card, and Darryl taking note of his interest in Dahlia was a point of consternation. His brother had read every card in his deck.

His sister Maitlyn asking questions was something else altogether. Once his sister began to pry into his business, she had reached a point of no return. The women in his family were never readily willing to give him or any of his brothers a break when it came to other women in their lives.

Darryl going out of his way to comment on Dahlia meant his brother had taken note of much more than Guy would have liked. He himself wasn't quite ready to acknowledge his sudden interest in the beautiful woman.

Since their first meeting, the encounter in her office and agreeing to take the role in her movie, Guy had invested a lot of energy in discovering everything he could about Dahlia. He'd even broken one of his cardinal rules, calling up the friend of a friend of a friend, who'd allegedly dated Dahlia, to discreetly inquire about her. Everything he'd discovered said that she was a woman devoted to her craft, loyal to a fault and not at all caught up in the shallow facade of what a Hollywood powerhouse was expected to be.

Everyone he'd spoken to had only favorable things to say about Dahlia, not one individual cosigning the tabloid fodder that had been written about her in the past. And much had been written about Dahlia; the supermarket rags read like the gossip bible of all things Dahlia Morrow. But even the tabloids didn't dispute her talents as a filmmaker, and that in and of itself provoked much thought. Guy was thinking that the exquisite and enigmatic Dahlia Morrow was a woman he really wanted to get to know better.

Chapter 5

Matthew, Mark, Luke and John Stallion were seated around the family breakfast table when their sister, Phaedra, made her way into the family home. The four brothers greeted her warmly as she rounded the table, planting kisses on each of their cheeks. Phaedra still marveled at the emotion that bubbled within her each time she was in their presence. Just months earlier she hadn't had a clue about their existence, and now she was celebrating the joy of having brothers who cared about her well-being and family that loved her unconditionally. Discovering her link to the Stallion lineage had been a whirlwind experience, but she now found herself forever a Stallion, and she loved everything that represented.

"Welcome home," John, her oldest brother, said as he gestured for her to take a seat at the table beside him.

"Where's that new husband of yours?" Mark asked casually, his gaze turned toward the doorway.

"He's headed to the office. Something about the property in Geneva having problems with their front office upgrade," she said with a shrug of her shoulders.

Luke, the youngest of the Stallion brothers, nodded knowingly. "Geneva's been a problem from start to finish. I'm hoping Mason can work his magic for us," he said as he rose to his feet. He tossed his cloth napkin on the table. "I need to meet with him so that we can see if we can get this thing going." Luke excused himself and exited the room.

Matthew glanced down at the watch on his wrist. "I have to run, as well, but when you get a chance, Phaedra, I need you to stop by my office. Our petition for your name change has been approved by the courts, and we just need to file the final paperwork to insure that all your legal documents reflect your new moniker."

Mark eyed her curiously, his gaze sweeping around the table. "You changed your name?"

Phaedra nodded. "Yep! I guess I am officially Phaedra Stallion-Boudreaux now."

John nodded his approval, which made Phaedra smile. As the patriarch of their small family, he was very opinionated about everything his siblings did, and Phaedra was no exception. His endorsement meant the world to her, and she found herself seeking out his opinion on most of her decisions, even her recent marriage to Mason Boudreaux.

Matthew leaned in to kiss her forehead before he headed for the door, Mark following close on his heels.

"Katrina is upstairs with Jack," Matthew said, referring to his wife and newborn son. "She said for you not to leave without coming up to see her. Something about the christening," he said as he saluted them goodbye.

The familial connection with her brother being married to her husband's sister was a source of great joy to her, and every time she thought about it she found herself smiling.

"So what's on your agenda today?" John asked, his booming voice pulling at her attention.

"I was hoping to get your opinion on an investment," Phaedra said, passing a prospectus in his direction.

With eyebrows raised, John took a moment to review the documents inside, leaning forward as he spread everything out before him. As Phaedra waited, she reached for one of the toasted bagels that rested on a ceramic platter in the center of the table, then slathered it with jalapeño-flavored cream cheese. By her third bite John was tapping numbers into a calculator application on his iPad. His expression was blank, and Phaedra was unable to get a read on what her big brother was thinking. By the time John was done, Phaedra was working on her second bagel, a bowl of fresh fruit and a third cup of coffee.

"So what do you think?" she queried when he finally placed the documents inside their manila folder and sat back in his seat.

He hesitated for a brief moment before responding. "Tell me why this project?" he asked.

"The filmmaker is a dear friend and sorority sister of mine."

"Dahlia Morrow?"

"Correct. Dahlia and I went to school together. We've been the best of friends since the first day we met. We pledged together, and I love her to pieces. Dahlia is good at what she does. This script is one that is near and dear to her heart, and if anyone can bring it to the big screen and turn it into a box office sensation, Dahlia can. She needs help to get there, though, and I really want to help her. But I want to be smart about it, too."

"Didn't she just win an Oscar or something?" John asked.

Phaedra nodded. "Her last film, *Victory's Daughter,* was nominated for seven Oscars and took Best Picture. Dahlia is the youngest and the first black woman to win an Oscar for Best Director."

"And she has high hopes for this film. What's it called again?"

"*Passionate,* after the name of the lead female character."

"Has she cast her leads yet?"

"Zahara Ginolfi has signed on to play the part of Passionate."

"Wow," John exclaimed. "She's good, and she has a huge following," he said of the Grammy-winning songstress turned award-winning actress. "I'm impressed. What about the leading man?"

Phaedra grinned. "She just signed Mason's brother," she said excitedly.

John laughed. "*The* Guy Boudreaux! The black Bond himself. Very nice."

"So should I invest?" Phaedra asked again, her confidence boosted by her brother's enthusiasm.

John hesitated a second time, resting his elbows against the table and his chin against his fists. His head waved ever so slightly. "This is a tough one," he started, meeting Phaedra's gaze. "If you didn't have a personal connection to the film I would probably advise against it.

"When people invest in films, it's the potential for a high return that's the draw, but it is such a big risk with way too many ifs for a novice investor. Movies only do well *if* it's a good script, *if* it has good acting, *if* it has good production value and *if* it strikes a chord with distributors. If you are able to get past a number of those issues, the film can do well, but you could still lose everything you put into it if the distribution deals fall short."

Phaedra nodded as she reflected on John's comments.

He continued, "I think that in this case, the key reason for you to invest has to be more important than the potential return. You obviously believe in the message of the film and in the filmmaker. You like and support the movie's producer and cast. I also get the impression that you like the glamour of being involved, an opportunity to bring attention to your own photography perhaps," he said as he gestured toward the requisite camera she always carried with her. "This is why I say go for it. Consider it a tax write-off like you would if you were giving to a charity. That way it can still benefit you if it doesn't work out."

"Thanks," Phaedra said, her excitement gleaming in her eyes. She threw her arms around her big brother's neck and kissed his cheek. "I really appreciate your opinion," she added.

John nodded, giving her a slight wink of his eye. "And after you stop by Matthew's office, swing by mine and pick up a check for Dahlia. We have to support our family," he said, his smile warming his dark face.

"I love you," she said as she hugged him a second time. "And I know that Dahlia will appreciate the support."

John laughed with her. "I love you, too," he said.

Phaedra tossed back the last of her coffee. "I need to go up and see those nieces and nephews of ours," she said as she set her mug back down on the table. "I need to see Marah, too. Is your wife upstairs?"

John shook his head. "No, Marah flew to New York this morning," he said. "She and her sisters are franchising their dating business, and she's meeting with some potential investors. She'll be back tomorrow."

Phaedra rose to her feet as she gave him a quick wave of her hand. "I'll catch her tomorrow, then," she said as she headed for the door. "And I'll catch up with you later!" She then headed for the second floor and the playroom, where the rest of the Stallion women and babies were gathered.

Chapter 6

Tears misted Dahlia's eyes as she disconnected the call on her cell phone. She and her friend Phaedra had been talking for almost an hour, the two women catching up with each other's busy lives. Discovering that Phaedra and her family were excited to invest in her movie had been the icing on the cake; Dahlia's financial woes were resolved and she could now turn her total focus to filming.

When Phaedra had first voiced an interest in buying into Dahlia's film, Dahlia had been more than ready to fly to Dallas to plead her case for all that *Passionate* was worth. But Phaedra had not needed her sales pitch. Phaedra, like Leslie, had been with her when the idea of *Passionate* had been conceived. Phaedra had brought her coffee and donuts in the middle of the night when she'd first written the screenplay. Phaedra had photographed her slumped over her computer many nights and captured Dahlia's obsession with the story on film. Phaedra's confidence in her had come on the heels of Guy's confidence, and the duo's support meant more than Dahlia could have begun to hope for.

She swiped at her eyes with the backs of her hands, willing away the tears that threatened to spill past her thick lashes. She refused to be emotional, determined to contain her excitement. She was waiting for Guy Boudreaux to arrive, and there was no way she was going to allow him to find her teary-eyed and emotive. Everything about her demeanor when she met with the man had to be as calm and as collected as she could possibly manage. There was no way that she would permit him to see her out of her usual full and total control. No way.

She glanced down at her watch, noting that they were minutes from seeing each other again. She could feel her heart racing at the prospect. She took a deep breath to stall her nerves. She couldn't begin to understand why he disturbed her in ways she didn't want. But he was the most mesmerizing man she had ever met.

She was only slightly startled when Guy suddenly slid his muscular frame into the booth beside her. Lost in thought, she'd not seen him enter the room and his sudden presence threw her for a momentary loop.

"Hey, you!" Dahlia exclaimed, fighting to temper the excitement in her voice as she eyed him up and down. The man was neatly dressed in khaki slacks and a navy polo shirt, with the length of his dreadlocks pulled back in a neat ponytail at the nape of his neck.

"Hey, yourself," Guy said, a wide grin spreading slowly across his face. "Did you miss me?"

Dahlia laughed. "Was I supposed to miss you?"

"I missed you," Guy answered, casually dropping his right arm around the back of the booth behind her shoulders.

Dahlia's expression spoke volumes; her narrowed eyes and deep scowl moved Guy to laugh.

"What? Don't you believe me?" he intoned.

"You're quite full of yourself, aren't you, Mr. Boudreaux?" Dahlia asked casually.

Before Guy could answer, their waitress, a thin brunette with deep, dark eyes and chiseled features, approached the table. "Hi, my name is Lisa, and I'll be your server today," she said, her Valley-girl drawl rolling off her tongue like sugary bubblegum.

"Hi, Lisa," Guy greeted her. "How are you today?" he asked, his broad grin spreading farther.

"It's a good day," she replied, recognition crossing her face. "How about you, Mr. Boudreaux?"

Guy nodded. "It's a great day here. Things good with you today, Dahlia?" he queried, devilment twinkling in his eyes as he turned to stare at her.

Dahlia cut an eye at him first, then lifted her gaze to stare at the waitress. It was obvious that Lisa was completely smitten by Guy Boudreaux. The woman's gaze was so lost on the handsome man that Dahlia mused it would be a miracle if she could even remember where she was and why she was there.

"Just great!" Dahlia said as she turned to meet his eyes. She couldn't help but smile back as Guy continued to grin sheepishly. She found his charm disarming and his humor infectious. Dahlia shook her head as she felt herself being consumed by his presence.

"Can I interest you two in an appetizer?" Lisa asked, her gaze moving from one to the other.

"No, thank you," Dahlia said. "I'm ready to order. I'll take the number twenty-three, the breast combo with candied yams, greens and cornbread."

"A woman with a healthy appetite," Guy exclaimed. "I like that."

Dahlia threw him a cheesy smile. "I just bet you do!" She lifted her gaze back to the young woman, who was eyeing them curiously. "And my friend here will have the chef salad. He's in training, getting ready for a big movie," she quipped.

"That's so exciting," Lisa exclaimed as she stared at Guy like a deer caught deep in headlights. There was an awkward moment of silence as Guy gazed back at her.

"Iced tea would really be good right about now, too," Dahlia intoned, pulling at the waitress's attention.

Lisa nodded quickly, turned an about-face and rushed off without saying another word.

Dahlia laughed. "I think she's a little starstruck. Two minutes from now she'll have to come back to ask you what kind of salad dressing you want," she said, predicting the question the young woman had failed to ask. She took a quick glance at her wristwatch.

"And what made you think that I wanted a salad?" Guy interjected. "I had my mouth primed for some chicken and waffles!"

"I'm sure you did," Dahlia said sarcastically as she

gestured toward the other side of the room. "Your friend Lisa is on her way back over, so you can change your order if you want."

The girl moved back to their table. "I'm sorry, but what kind of salad dressing would you like with your salad?" she asked, a befuddled expression crossing her face.

Dahlia chuckled softly to herself, imagining that if the poor girl could drop deep into a hole in the floor that she would, pulling in everything *except* Guy Boudreaux on top of herself. "That's no problem," she said, her tone soothing. "In fact, we apologize, but if it's not too much trouble my friend here has decided he would prefer chicken today. Mr. Boudreaux will have the number three instead—half a chicken with two waffles," she finished. "Thank you."

Lisa nodded. "Okay, so that's a number three, Southern-style?"

"Yes, please," Guy said. He leaned back in his seat, shaking his head as they watched the girl rush to the kitchen.

"Do all women have that kind of reaction around you?" Dahlia asked, laughing warmly. "Because that poor child has completely lost it."

Guy shrugged. "Obviously not. You don't seem to be falling apart."

"I'm not like other women."

Guy smiled, the bend of his full lips rising with glee. "No, you're not, are you? Actually, you're kind of bossy and controlling," he noted, tilting his head toward her.

Dahlia pulled her hands to her chest, her fingers resting against her clavicle. "Me? Controlling?" she said, her eyebrows raised.

Guy laughed. "And bossy!"

Dahlia smiled back as she suddenly became aware of the light graze of his fingers pressing against her bare skin; his arm was still wrapped around the back of the cushioned booth and her shoulders.

There was a pregnant pause as they sat studying each other, neither saying a word but both suddenly thinking the same thing. Whether they expressed the sentiment out loud or not, it had been clear from their very first encounter that something was brewing between them. It was the slight looks, the veiled hints and innuendoes, his hand touching her shoulder for a second longer than necessary— Those unspoken signals hinted at the promise of something exciting and provocative to come. Both were thinking it, and then they weren't, shaking the sensation away as quickly as it had risen.

Dahlia cleared her throat and took a second sip of her drink. "I haven't properly thanked you for the money you contributed to the film. I can't begin to tell you how much your generosity means to me."

"You're very welcome. Since I like the idea of being involved in more ways than just adding my acting chops, it seemed like a smart investment."

"Well, I appreciate it, and I appreciate you getting your family on board, as well."

Guy eyed her curiously, his eyebrows lifted in question. "My family?"

Dahlia met his gaze, surprised by his inquisitive stare. "Didn't you know? Phaedra and her husband,

Mason, made a very substantial investment. And so did Phaedra's brother, John Stallion."

"No, I didn't know," Guy answered, his head bobbing lightly against his broad shoulders. There was a pause as their lunch was delivered. Heat billowed off his plate of crispy, batter-fried chicken and buttermilk waffles. The decadent aromas wafted up his nostrils, the sweet scent reminding him of home and his family. As the waitress excused herself, he continued their conversation.

"So, how much more do you think you'll need to finish the film?"

"Not much at all. In fact, I'll be able to cover any additional expenses out of my personal funds. We can go ahead and begin shooting the film. We're in a really great place."

"And just so I'm clear, we'll be able to review your books, right?" Guy questioned as he lifted a forkful of food to his mouth.

Dahlia bristled ever so slightly. "Don't you trust me?"

Guy smiled, swiping at his lips with a paper napkin before he answered. "It's not about trust. It's about protecting my family's investment. I feel kind of responsible now. Why are you offended?"

"I'm not offended."

"Yes, you are."

Dahlia rolled her eyes. "No, I am not. You, Phaedra and your brother-in-law as well as anyone else who has invested a dollar in this movie will be able to review the books at any time. In addition, the accountant will send you quarterly updates on the expenditures."

Guy nodded, changing the subject. "You're an only child, aren't you?"

There was a second's pause as Dahlia reflected on his question. She thought briefly about the half brothers that she barely knew, her siblings who had been raised by their respective mothers on different sides of the country. As a little girl, there had been numerous cross-country trips with their father. Kent and Palmer, older than Dahlia by nine and ten years, had grown, and the trips had morphed into father-daughter jaunts by the time Dahlia had reached her twelfth birthday.

Through the years, the family had not done a great job of keeping in contact with one another, a fact that Dahlia had promised herself too many times she would rectify. She finally answered Guy's question, adding her own query. "No, I'm not, why would you ask?"

"Because you were a little sensitive when I asked about your books. You don't like anyone checking up behind you. You're not used to it. When you have brothers and sisters you kind of get used to someone watching you over your shoulder."

Dahlia shrugged. "I have two half brothers, but we're not very close. I haven't seen them in a few years although they do call every few months or so. But I wasn't at all being sensitive," she added defensively.

Guy nodded, a wry smile pulling at his full mouth. "There are nine of us, and we all speak to each other practically every day. One of us is always checking up behind one of the others. There is little that any of us do that all of us don't know about."

"Nine! Wow. Where do you fall in that mix?"

"There are five boys and four girls. I'm the eighth kid, the youngest boy."

"Wow," Dahlia exclaimed a second time. "I can't begin to imagine what that might be like."

Guy laughed. "Actually it's always been a lot of fun, sort of like having your own personal cheerleading squad. I don't think I'd want it any other way."

"I can understand that. I remember a lot of good times with my brothers. We had a lot of fun, and they were once very protective."

"So why haven't you made more of an effort to reconnect with them?"

"Excuse me?"

"You heard me. I didn't stutter," Guy said matter-of-factly.

Dahlia leaned back in her seat, her arms crossing in front of her. She was stunned by his audacity; his expression was just shy of being arrogant. She stammered slightly, searching for the right words to tell him her business was, and would always be, none of his. But Guy spoke before she did.

"Before you get yourself all worked up, the point I was trying to make is that if you want things to change you have to make the effort for them to do so. My mother would tell you that talking about it won't make it happen. Doing about it will."

Dahlia took a deep breath, still eyeing him with reservation as he gestured for the waitress. Despite being completely annoying, every time the man smiled, the brilliance of it like a spotlight on her spirit, she couldn't help but like him more.

"Would you like some dessert?" Lisa asked, staring at Guy and completely avoiding Dahlia's gaze. Her expression spoke volumes. He laughed loudly, completely amused.

Just as Dahlia leaned forward to speak, Guy lifted his hand and waved his index finger in front of her, stalling her words as he ordered for them. "Lisa, we will take a very, very large slice of the best cake you have back there with two scoops of vanilla ice cream on top and two spoons, please."

"Will that be all?" the waitress asked as she jotted the order down on a slip of paper.

"And the check, please," Dahlia added, taking a quick glance down at her cell phone.

When Lisa was out of earshot, Guy slid closer toward her, leaning in as if he was going to whisper something. As he drew his face close to hers, the distinctive scent of Acqua di Gio teased her nostrils.

"Are you still mad?" he questioned, that damn smile sending a shimmer of electricity straight through her core.

Dahlia met his stare, her own smile widening across her face. "Yeah," she finally managed to mutter. "'Cause you should have ordered chocolate ice cream."

"I would have ordered both, but I'm training for a new movie, remember?" Guy smiled. When the ice cream and cake arrived with two spoons jutting from opposite ends of the glass bowl, he slid it between them, shifting his body even closer to hers as he did. Dahlia's eyes widened as his hip and leg slid against hers, and her breath caught in her throat at the nearness of him. She fought the urge to pull away, to slide her body from his, wanting to stall the sudden rise of heat threatening to consume her. Instead, she reached for the closest spoon and shoveled a serving of dessert into her mouth.

Neither spoke as they shared the decadent confection, both lost in thoughts of each other and reveling in the simplicity of the moment. Two hours later, the couple was still sitting side by side. With full stomachs they'd been talking nonstop, sharing stories about their childhoods, their ambitions, the movie and every other topic that happened to cross their minds in the moment. Both were comfortable, as if the time they shared was something they'd been doing every day for all of their lives.

Around them the dinner crowd was beginning to settle in for the evening meal. It was later than either of them could imagine, both enjoying the time they were spending together. The waitress had stopped frequently to refill their glasses, anxious to keep Guy satisfied for as long as he wanted to take up space at her table. And although they'd been interrupted a time or two by people seeking Guy's autograph, they'd gotten themselves so lost in each other that they'd frequently forgotten that they were sitting in a crowded room and not somewhere private.

Dahlia reached for the last glass of iced tea the waitress had deposited on the tabletop. She lifted her gaze to his as he sat staring intently at her, and something like longing shimmered between them. The feeling was startling, and Dahlia felt the rise of perspiration dampen her palms and puddle between her breasts.

She was suddenly quivering with excitement, grateful for the seat beneath her bottom. The man had ignited a fire in the core of her feminine spirit; heat rose like wildfire from the center of her being. Desire surged, and Dahlia was suddenly hungry for something she'd not even known she needed. Like day needed night to be complete. Like one needed oxygen to breathe.

She found herself wishing that their time together would never end, and her eyes widened at the absurdity. Shaking with emotion, she gestured toward Lisa for the check that she'd forgotten to bring.

Guy cleared his throat, fighting to stall the rise of heat that had suddenly consumed him, as well. Guy wanted her, and he didn't want her like he wanted a cup of coffee or wanted to get an extra ten minutes of sleep. He wanted Dahlia like a man twenty feet under water with a cement block chained to his ankles wanted air. He wanted her like a skydiver with a bad rip cord wants his parachute to open. His want of Dahlia felt soul-deep, obsessive and carnal, like nothing he'd ever known before.

"This one's on me," Guy said as he reached to take the tab from Dahlia's hand.

She pulled it back and shook her head as she passed it and her credit card to the waitress. "No way," she stated emphatically. "And have you talking about me later? I don't think so." She smiled brightly.

Guy chuckled. "Yeah, I would talk about you. I almost regret what I told people about you and that bottle of water from our casting meeting yesterday," he said, shaking his head. "Almost."

"See. I've got your number," Dahlia said. She was still grinning from ear to ear.

"Well, let me leave the tip, then," Guy said as he reached into the pocket of his slacks and pulled out his billfold.

As Dahlia signed the credit card receipt and handed it back to Lisa, Guy slipped a hundred-dollar bill into the young girl's hands. Lisa's eyes bulged with appreciation.

"Thank you," she exclaimed excitedly. "Thank you so much!"

Guy winked at her as she rushed back to share the news of her good fortune with her coworkers.

Dahlia rose to her feet. "This was nice," she said. "I had a really good time."

"So did I," Guy said, walking her out the restaurant and guiding her in the direction of her vehicle. "It's probably been one of the best first dates that I've ever had."

She cut her eye at him as he took her car keys from her hands and unlocked the car for her. He opened the door and gestured for her to get inside. She stood her ground, shaking her head vehemently.

"This was not a first date," she said as she snatched her keys from his fingers.

Guy nodded, his laugh teasing. "Yes. It was. This was definitely a first date."

"No. It wasn't," Dahlia stated emphatically. Then Guy slipped his arm around her waist, his palm pressed firmly against her lower back and pulled her tightly to him. The gesture stalled her protests somewhere in her throat, and her eyes widened in surprise as Guy leaned in and pressed a damp kiss against her cheek.

"I'm flying to New York tomorrow to finish filming my Chanel commercial. We can plan our second date for when I get back. I'll give you a call."

Guy kissed her cheek a second time before releasing the hold he had on her. "Stay safe," he said as he took her by the elbow and guided her inside her car. He winked as he secured the door, then turned and headed in the direction of his own car.

Through all of it Dahlia was in a state of flux, her head bouncing up and down like a bobblehead doll. "I don't date," she finally managed to muster, the comment echoing inside the closed vehicle as Guy Boudreaux disappeared from her sight.

Chapter 7

The sound of the telephone ringing pulled Guy from a deep sleep, and his body quivered with sweat. The waking was unexpected, and unwelcome, and the sensual dream he was experiencing left him so quickly that he suddenly felt lost, unable to get his bearings. He was surrounded by darkness. Nothing but the pale green glow of the digital clock illuminated the room. He rolled onto his stomach to reach across the nightstand for his cell phone. When he knocked the device to the floor he cursed under his breath.

His member was rock-hard, a rod of steel pressing hot against his leg. He rolled over onto his back as he clasped the length of himself in the palm of his hand. He'd been thinking about Dahlia since he'd left her side a few days ago; the warmth of her skin still burned hot against his lips. He hadn't been able to get her off his mind, thinking of her during his flight to New York and as he'd completed his photo shoot. Now she was tripping through his dreams, the sensual fantasy so real that he was still hard with desire for the luscious woman.

When his phone beeped, indicating someone had left him a voice mail, he was still thinking about her, his hand still wrapped tightly around his sex as he stroked himself gently. Guy blew a deep sigh past his lips as he rolled back over and reached for the light on the nightstand. He turned it on, then collected his cell phone from the floor. The message light blinked rapidly. Dialing his mailbox, he pulled the device to his ear and listened.

"Guy, hey, this is Dahlia." There was a moment's pause as if she was collecting her thoughts before moving on. "I wasn't sure when you planned to be back from New York, but I needed to start scheduling script run-throughs and rehearsal times. I wasn't sure if you did your own scheduling or if you had an assistant, so I figured I'd call you myself so that I could also thank you for lunch the other day, too. Well…okay then…I guess I will just catch up with you later."

Guy smiled broadly, a sense of knowing spreading through his body. Dahlia had a very adept staff who handled her tasks; he knew she didn't call to do scheduling, and she knew that all of his scheduling was done through his agent's office. But he could hear what she really wanted. He could hear it in her voice—the inflection of her words betrayed her. Dahlia Morrow couldn't get him off her mind, either.

Rolling back against the mattress, he sighed. He liked her. But dating the woman who'd employed him was not the smartest thing he could do. Nor did it make sense to date a woman with a reputation like Dahlia's. He could just imagine the problems on set if things didn't work out between them and the scandal that would send the tabloids into a gossip overload. He also had no interest in just being another trophy on Dahlia Morrow's romantic shelf. As he had heard it, Dahlia had collected a number of trophies since arriving on the West Coast. The more he thought about it, the more certain he was that her and him together would not be a wise business decision, and Guy was determined to make wiser decisions about his career.

As he lay pondering his options, Guy thought it best that he leave things strictly professional between the two of them. But the raging erection that persisted as thoughts of the woman ran through his mind kept telling him something wholeheartedly different.

"You wanted to start scheduling? Really, Dahlia?" Leslie let out a slight laugh.

"Shut up, Leslie," her friend said as she dropped her head into her hands. "I sounded like a complete idiot."

Leslie nodded. "You sounded…well…sort of…stalkerlike, actually.…"

Dahlia cut an evil eye at the woman. "This is all your fault. I don't know why I listen to you. I never should have called that man."

"You needed to call that man so that I can stop hearing you complain about that kiss he gave you."

Dahlia was still shaking her head, still in awe of Guy's audacity. He had kissed her, and the gesture had completely thrown her off balance. He had some nerve, she thought to herself. She then voiced her chagrin for the umpteenth time. "Can you believe he had the nerve to kiss me?"

"It was your cheek, Dahlia," Leslie countered, tossing her hands in the air. "Your cheek! Had he really laid one on you then you might have had something to complain about."

"Still," Dahlia said. "It was *my* cheek and I didn't want him kissing any part of my body."

Leslie laughed. "Oh, yes, you did! Your problem is you wished he had given you a real kiss. You wanted him to bust one on you good and he didn't."

Dahlia didn't bother to look in her friend's direction. She didn't want Leslie to see the look on her face because Leslie would see she *had* wanted Guy to kiss her and she had wanted to kiss him back. But everything about the two of them was so out of character for her that she didn't even know where to begin to get things right.

Dahlia needed to get herself back on track when it came to Guy Boudreaux. A dalliance with Guy wasn't going to move her career forward, in fact, it was possible that another tabloid rumor about her and one more man might send her professional career careening right off the edge of legitimacy. Dahlia knew that there were those who already viewed her with a wary eye, earnestly believing that she did nothing more than jump from one man to another, leaping from bed to bed like a frog in heat. She decided that whatever was brewing between her and Guy had to quickly come to a screeching halt before it snowballed out of control.

She sighed deeply. She reached a manicured hand to her cheek, her fingers caressing where his lips had rested, the round tips of her nails gliding along her profile. She bit down against her bottom lip.

It had been some time since a man had really kissed her, his lips laying claim to her lips, every hard muscle of his body in sync with hers. Instinctively, she knew that Guy was a man who'd be in total sync with her. The nearness of him caused her to break out into a full sweat, perspiration pooling in places moisture had no business being. Closing her eyes, she couldn't stop herself from thinking about Guy kissing her mouth, then caressing, kneading and teasing every ounce of her sensibilities.

Opening her eyes, Dahlia fanned herself with her hand, heat rising with a vengeance. From the office entrance Leslie laughed heartily, and the two women locked gazes. Not saying another word, Leslie made her exit, still chuckling with glee. Glancing down at the watch on her wrist, Dahlia was suddenly struck by the difference in time between California and New York. She had no doubts that Guy was probably sound asleep in bed. And then she couldn't stop herself from wondering what it might be like to be in bed with him.

Chapter 8

Maitlyn Boudreaux Parks leaned back in her seat, her arms folded over her chest and her legs crossed out in front of her. She was staring hard at her brother Guy. "Don't ignore me," she said sternly.

"I'm not ignoring you, Maitlyn. I'm ignoring your question," Guy said, pretending to study the dinner menu in his hands.

"Why?" his sister queried. "It's an easy question to answer. Is there something going on with you and Dahlia Morrow?"

Guy sighed. "No," he said firmly.

Maitlyn's eyes narrowed slightly as she continued to stare at him. "But you want something to be going on with the two of you?"

"I didn't say that," Guy answered, finally dropping

his menu on the table and meeting her intense stare. "Why are you bothering me about her?"

"I'm not bothering you. Paparazzi shot you and Dahlia dining together, and people are asking questions. A newspaper columnist even called to ask if we had a comment about your alleged relationship."

"And you told them…?"

"I told them that you recently signed to do her next movie and that you're very excited about the project. Don't worry—I didn't infer that there was anything personal going on between you two."

"Then you done good," Guy said, his signature smile beaming at her.

"But I want to know the truth," his sister persisted. "Are you two sleeping together?"

"No!" Guy said emphatically, a rush of color flooding his face. "And if we were, I wouldn't tell you."

"I'm your manager and your agent. I would need to know."

"You're also my family, and, no, you don't need to know."

Maitlyn smiled. "Fine. I'll just ask Dahlia."

Guy's eyes widened. "Don't you dare!"

His sister laughed heartily. "I thought so!"

Guy laughed with her. "Leave me alone, Mattie. If you have to know, we went to lunch one time. It was a very nice afternoon. And, yes, I am hoping that she and I can have a few more nice times together. Happy?"

"No. Dahlia Morrow has a reputation for breaking men's hearts. I've lost count of the number of men that she's been linked to. I don't want to see you get hurt."

Reaching for his sister's hand, Guy tapped the back of it gently. "I appreciate the concern, but I've got this under control, thank you very much." He changed the subject. "So, what's up with you and Donald?" he asked, referring to his sister's estranged husband. "You two make up yet?"

Maitlyn let out a sigh of her own. "We just can't seem to find our balance together anymore. It's really sad," she said, her thoughts suddenly flooded with the issues that were rapidly disintegrating her marriage.

Guy tapped her hand again. "It'll work itself out. Darryl's having issues with Asia, too, you know."

Maitlyn rolled her eyes. "That girl is crazy! He should have cut her loose months ago. Even Mommy says he needs to let her go."

Guy chuckled. "And what did Mommy say about me and Dahlia?"

His sister laughed with him, noting the hint of sarcasm in his tone. "Mommy said it's about time," she answered.

Shaking his head, Guy gestured for the waiter to take their dinner orders. The siblings continued to catch up, enjoying their late-night meal. When all was done, they exited the hotel's dining room and headed back to their respective rooms.

"What time is your flight tomorrow?" Guy asked, holding the elevator door open as Maitlyn stepped out onto the fifteenth floor.

"I'm here for an additional day, actually," Maitlyn answered, turning to face Guy. "The Giorgio Armani Group is interested in you representing a new collection they have coming out. I told them I'd take a meeting to see what they're offering."

Guy nodded. "Do you need me to stay?"

His sister shook her head. "No. Besides, I know how anxious you are to get back to Los Angeles…and Dahlia."

"Thanks," he said warmly. "I appreciate that."

"Don't thank me. Thank Mommy. She told me to stay out of you and Dahlia's way!"

As the elevator door closed between them, Guy laughed happily. He definitely loved his family.

Once the door was closed to his hotel suite, Guy stepped out of his clothes, folding them neatly before he dropped them into the bottom of his empty suitcase. He had a long list of things he needed to do, including packing for his early morning flight, yet all he could think about was Dahlia. He'd been doing well keeping her out of his thoughts, and then his sister had reawakened his memories of her. Dahlia Morrow haunted him like a too-sweet spirit. And now his mother and sisters were discussing the two of them as if they were already a couple. He had to laugh at the absurdity.

He hadn't returned her telephone call yet. Instead, he'd passed her message on to Maitlyn for her to handle. He hadn't returned her telephone call because he didn't want Dahlia to think that he was anxious because he was anxious. Although he enjoyed the initial flirtations between them, he was not enjoying the flood of emotions that seemed to come when Dahlia was on his mind. He was looking forward to seeing her again, for them to spend time together and for the two of them to get to know each other even better. Guy wasn't willing to admit it, but Dahlia Morrow had his interest peaked. And Guy, not knowing how far he wanted to take it, wasn't ready for her to know that just yet.

Dahlia was not accustomed to being ignored by any man. And, most assuredly, she wasn't accustomed to being ignored by a man she was interested in. She scanned the call log on her smartphone for the umpteenth time, checking once again that she had not missed Guy's return call. And once again there was nothing from him. No text message, no missed call, no voice mail message, nothing. One whole week of nothing, and Dahlia wasn't happy about that fact. She definitely wasn't happy that she cared so much. Tossing the phone onto the end table, Dahlia watched as it slid across the table's polished surface and dropped down onto the floor. She sighed deeply, a slight pout pulling at her mouth. It was bothering her that she was feeling anything at all about Guy Boudreaux, because Dahlia never felt much of anything for any man. Filmmaking had always been her only passion and very little else excited her. But suddenly wanting Guy was really beginning to take its toll.

What she needed, Dahlia thought, was a diversion. Something else to occupy her thoughts instead of the lurid fantasies she'd been having about her and Guy together. Because she'd been having some very vivid thoughts, and all of them had centered on his kisses.

There had been something in his touch, something heated and intoxicating. The gentle graze of his fingertips against her skin had left her hungry, her body suddenly craving more. Every time she thought about him and his lips pressed hot against her cheek, she imagined his hands teasing her goodies as she offered him her sugar and sweets. Dahlia pressed her knees tightly together, anxious to stall the rise of wanting that seemed to suddenly cry out for attention.

She exhaled loudly, then dropped down onto her hands and knees to retrieve her phone from beneath the table. Sitting back in her chair, she hesitated for a brief moment as she pondered her options. And then she dialed. An hour later, dressed to the nines, Dahlia answered her front door and welcomed her friend Drake Houston inside.

Chapter 9

Laughter rang loudly through the stretch limo. The five Boudreaux brothers, Guy, Kendrick, Donovan, Darryl and Mason, enjoyed a good time together.

"Glad you guys could pick me up from the airport." Guy said, leaning back in his seat, glad to be back in Los Angeles.

Mason nodded. "So, whose bright idea was this, anyway?" he asked.

Darryl laughed. "We all just figured you needed to have a proper bachelor party. Even if we are having it *after* the wedding." He popped the cork on a bottle of champagne and began to fill five glasses.

Mason laughed with him. "Uh, sure, but I know that this is not about me. Try again, little brother!"

Donovan shook his head. "Actually, with everything

we all have going on in the next few months it seemed like a good time for us to spend some quality time together. You and Darryl are headed to New Orleans to kick off your new project. Guy starts filming his movie. I'll be starting my dissertation and Kendrick…well…I don't know what Kendrick's going to be doing."

"I don't know what I'm doing, either," Kendrick interjected, "but I know I'll be busy."

Guy shook his head. "Well, it's good we could spend some time together. And I'm glad you all made the effort to come to me this time."

"Without the girls," Donovan added.

"Definitely without the girls!" the other brothers echoed, lifting their champagne glasses in salute.

"Speaking of our sisters, any one of you talk to Maitlyn lately?" Guy asked. "'Cause she's going through something but she's not talking to me."

"Same story, different day. Donald's not making their separation easy," Mason said softly. "I spoke to her yesterday, and he's asked her for a divorce and wants to sue her for the house."

"Son of a…" Guy muttered beneath his breath.

"She doesn't need the house," Donovan said.

"No, she doesn't, and I told her to let him buy her out, move on and be done with the whole mess," Mason responded. "She doesn't need the drama."

"Someone needs to bust Donald in his—" Kendrick started.

"Uh, she doesn't need that, either," Mason interjected, stalling his brother's thought. "Maitlyn needs to pray on the whole mess, and we need to pray for her and support whatever she wants to do."

Kendrick rolled his dark eyes.

"Well, I'll call her tomorrow and check on her," Donovan said.

"We all will," Darryl said. "And since we're talking about love lives, how are you and your woman doing?" he asked, shifting in his seat to meet Guy's gaze.

His brother eyed him with annoyance. "I don't have a woman, thank you."

"That's not what we heard," Kendrick piped in.

Guy shook his head. "And what did you hear?"

His brothers all laughed. "You know there are no secrets in this family," Mason said. "Each of your sisters has called to fill each of us in on you and your movie-star love interest."

"She's a filmmaker, not a movie star, and I'm still considering my options," Guy answered.

Darryl laughed. "He's scared."

"Scared of what?" Guy quizzed. "Brother, please!"

"Mmm-hmm. He's scared," Donovan chimed in. "I heard she's been around the block a few times. They say your filmmaker is a real heartbreaker."

Guy bristled, a wave of tension tightening his muscles. "I don't care what you heard," he insisted. "She's not like that." He then quickly changed the subject. "Speaking of heartbreakers, how are Katrina and our new nephew?" he asked, turning toward Mason.

Mason chuckled as he tapped his iPhone, pulling up his images. A recent photo of baby Matthew Jacoby Stallion Junior filled the screen. "Baby Jack is too cute for words! And Katrina is enjoying every minute of motherhood, again."

"I need to get to Dallas to see them and spend some time with Collin," Kendrick said, thinking of his older nephew. "He's at that age!"

Mason nodded. "He is, but Matthew is really keeping him in check. In fact, all of the Stallion brothers have been a great influence on him."

"That boy doesn't know yet just how lucky he is to have so much family to support him," Guy noted.

"He'll learn," Kendrick said matter-of-factly. "The first time his aunts get all in his business, he'll learn."

"I heard that," Darryl said. "Just ask Guy."

The brothers laughed heartily.

"Well, we're here," Guy stated. "Let's go eat well, drink much and have a good time!"

"Where is here?" Mason asked, peering out the tinted windows.

Guy grinned. "Spago!"

Dahlia was enjoying the crowd at Spago restaurant. Many familiar faces were there, enjoying their meals and having a great time. Her dinner companion was being overly attentive—as usual Drake hoped that he might get lucky whenever he and Dahlia shared a night on the town.

Dahlia hated to burst his happy bubble but not even the wine he was plying her with was going to move her to ever sleep with him. Besides, her hopes were that the time out would get her mind off Guy Boudreaux. But she was still thinking about him and fantasizing about the two of them together. She let out an audible sigh.

"Is everything okay, Dahlia? You look sad," Drake asked, concern crossing his face.

Dahlia raised her eyebrows but smiled brightly. "Everything's fine, Drake. I'm having a great time."

Drake grinned broadly, leaning over to plant a kiss against her cheek. His lips were dry and chapped, feeling like sandpaper against her flesh. She struggled not to wince from the sensation, clenching her teeth tightly as her lips pulled into a wider smile. She gripped her wineglass in her fist and took a big gulp, then gestured for the waiter to bring them another bottle.

Across the room Guy spied her as he and his brothers were being led to their table. Taking note of the well-known actor kissing her cheek, he felt himself bristle, something like jealousy striking a chord across his spirit. His sudden tension did not go unnoticed.

"What's up?" Mason questioned as he walked by Guy's side. He looked over to where his brother stared. "Everything okay?"

Guy nodded, shaking off the sensation as he met his brother's eyes. "It's all good," he said, his tone indicating otherwise.

"Hey, isn't that your woman?" Darryl suddenly interrupted, pointing in Dahlia's direction.

"I don't have a woman," Guy said, turning an about-face.

"No, really, isn't that Dahlia Morrow?" Darryl persisted.

"Sit down, Darryl," Guy said.

Guy's brothers chuckled as they took their seats at the table.

Kendrick leaned toward Darryl, gesturing with his head. "Which one is she?"

"The cutie in the corner," Darryl answered.

"With that actor from that comedy show? What's his name?"

"Yeah, her. He's Drake something or other."

"Can we change the subject, please?" Guy said as he gestured for their waitress.

Mason laughed, his gaze shifting from one brother to the other. "You guys cut Guy some slack. That woman is obviously a sensitive subject for him."

Kendrick laughed with him. "I'd be sensitive, too, if my woman was cuddled up with some other guy."

"She's not my woman," Guy snapped.

"With the way old boy is slobbering on her, I'd say not," Donovan noted, pointing with his index finger. "Your girl has been known to get around."

Guy turned to where his brother pointed, eyeing Drake just as he kissed Dahlia's cheek again and nuzzled his face into her neck. A rush of heat pricked him a second time. "Don't talk about her like that," he said through clenched teeth.

Before any of the brothers could comment further, their waitress appeared at the table, eager to serve.

Across the room Dahlia rose from her seat, heading to the restroom to wipe Drake's touch from her face. As she spun around she couldn't help but notice the table of diners seated across the way, five handsome black men laughing heartily among themselves. Their famil-

iarity drew her attention, and she paused, trying to rec-
ollect where she might know one or more of them from.

Her gaze skated around the table, and recognition
came when she locked gazes with Guy Boudreaux, who
turned to stare intently in her direction. Seeing him
face-to-face took her breath her away, and for a brief
moment Dahlia thought that her quivering knees might
send her straight to the floor. Taking a deep breath, she
smiled, wishing suddenly that she could disappear to
parts unknown. But with nowhere to go, she headed in
his direction instead, a bright smile painted on her face.

"Guy, hello!" Dahlia trilled as she moved to his side.
She nodded in greeting, tossing a warm smile to the
other men seated with him. "Gentlemen, good evening."

Guy rose from his seat. "Dahlia, what a surprise,"
he said politely as he shook her extended hand. "Are
you here alone?"

Behind him Darryl and Kendrick locked gazes,
fighting not to laugh out loud.

"No," Dahlia said softly. "Drake Houston and I were
just grabbing a late dinner." She gestured toward the
table she'd just vacated. "When did you get back from
New York?"

Guy shrugged his shoulders ever so slightly. "I just
landed actually. My brothers picked me up from the
airport."

"Oh, this is your family," Dahlia gushed, looking
around the table.

"I'm sorry. How rude of me," Guy said as he pointed
with his index finger. "Dahlia, these are my brothers.

This is Mason, Donovan, Darryl and Kendrick. Guys, this is Dahlia Morrow."

Each of the brothers stood up, extending their hands to shake Dahlia's. "It's very nice to meet you all," she said, noting their stark resemblance.

There was no escaping the Boudreaux lineage. Their distinctive features hinted of an African-Asian ancestry, with their slight angular eyes, thin noses, high cheek lines and full, pouty lips. Side by side they were a kaleidoscope of colorations that ranged from burnt umber to milk chocolate.

Guy was more bohemian in styling than his brothers with the dreads that hung well past his broad shoulders and the casual jeans and black T-shirt he wore. Guy's brothers Donovan and Mason could have passed for twins; the low lines of their closely cropped haircuts complemented their distinctive facial features and conservative attire. Kendrick sported a full, shaped Afro and boasted a deviant, bad-boy facade in his low-slung, tattered jeans, leather vest and high-priced sneakers.

They were each beautiful specimens of maleness, and as Dahlia stood in their presence she was suddenly aware of all the attention they were getting from the female patrons in the room. Only one of them had her full attention, though. Her gaze moved back to Guy. She took a deep breath, inhaling the familiar scent of his cologne.

For a brief moment there was an awkward pause at the two stood staring at each other. Dahlia then cleared her throat. "You didn't call me," she said, a hint of attitude in her tone.

Guy shrugged, contrition gleaming from his dark eyes. "Sorry about that. I just…well…it…" he sputtered, seemingly unable to form a coherent sentence.

Dahlia nodded. "What had happened was…" she said, mimicking him. She eyed him with a raised eyebrow.

At a loss for words, Guy could only shrug, a hangdog expression crossing his face. He grinned sheepishly.

Dahlia rolled her eyes. She then turned her attention back to the four brothers, who were watching them like one might watch a tennis match. "Well, it was very nice to meet you all," she said, her warm smile washing over each of them. She turned back to Guy, and her polite tone unnerved him. "It was good to see you again, Guy," she said softly. "Enjoy your dinner, gentlemen."

Guy nodded. "It was good to see you, too, Dahlia," he muttered in reply.

All eyes followed her closely as she exited the space, moving quickly toward the ladies' room. The Hérve Léger bandage dress she wore fit her to a T, the signature bands hugging her curves like a permanent tattoo. Every eye was glued to the sway of her small waist and full hips and the long length of her legs that stood on four-inch peep-toe pumps.

Across the table Kendrick hummed, a wide grin filling his brown face. "Mmm. I'd hit that," he exclaimed. "If you're not interested, I certainly could be."

"Shut up, Kendrick," Guy snapped.

His brothers laughed.

"Yeah, he's got it bad," Kendrick said.

"She's quite a beauty, Guy. And if I do say so myself, I think she likes you, too," Mason added.

Guy sighed deeply. "I… She…" he stammered, still awed by the wave of emotion that had suddenly consumed him. He dropped back into his seat and said nothing at all.

"And you're resisting that why again?" Donovan asked.

Guy tossed him a look. "I'm just taking my time. We'll be working together, and I really don't want to mix business with pleasure."

Mason nodded. "I can understand that. You don't want it to get messy."

"Exactly," Guy continued. "Especially since you and Phaedra have invested your money in this film, along with Phaedra's brother. I can't risk Dahlia and I falling out with each other and things not working between us and then the movie being compromised. It just wouldn't work."

"Who are you trying to convince, us or yourself?" Darryl queried.

Guy stared off to the side as he wasn't exactly sure of that himself.

Mason noted Guy's distress. "Just a friendly word of advice," he said softly, patting his brother on his back. "If you're truly interested in this woman, don't let the fear of what could happen keep you from pursuing her. She may very well be the one, but you won't know that if you don't take the chance. Step out on faith."

"I'll toast to that," Donovan said, lifting his glass in salute.

The other brothers joined him, lifting their glasses, as well. As they each took a sip of their beverages Dahlia made her way back across the room. She and Guy locked gazes as she passed, both holding their breath at the anticipation simmering beneath the surface between them. Dahlia gave him a slight smile and Guy responded with a deep nod of his head. He continued watching her as she sashayed past, rejoining Drake at their table. There was no missing Drake's excitement at her return.

Guy stiffened as he eyed the couple intently. He grabbed the drink that sat on the table before him and chugged a deep swig of the liquor. Whether he admitted it or not, he'd missed Dahlia more than he'd realized. And he was kicking himself for not having returned her phone call.

As Drake dropped an arm around Dahlia's shoulder, Guy felt himself bristle again, jealousy definitely coursing through his body. Suddenly aware of his brothers watching him watch her, he glanced around the table, his face flushed with color.

"Step out on faith," Mason said again as he reached for the basket of bread resting on the table.

Before he realized what he was doing, Guy stood up. He paused for a brief moment, then found himself moving in Dahlia's direction, coming to a halt at her table. He extended his hand toward her dinner companion. "Drake, how are you?"

Drake eyed him warily before returning the gesture, the two men shaking hands. "Guy. Guy Boudreaux. It's good to see you."

"You, as well," Guy responded. "I hate to interrupt you two, but, Dahlia, may I speak to you for a quick minute?" His stare was intense, his tone demanding.

His commanding presence shot a current of electricity up Dahlia's spine. "Oh, so now you have something you want to say to me," Dahlia said, still determined to give him a difficult time.

"Please," Guy persisted. "It's important."

Dahlia hesitated. "I don't think now is a good—"

Guy extended his hand, determined not to take no for an answer. "Now, Dahlia," he said sternly.

Her eyes widened. "Well…I…" Dahlia stammered as she moved to her feet, sliding her slim body past Drake and out of the booth they occupied. "Is something wrong?" she questioned, concern washing over her expression.

"No," Guy replied as he suddenly slipped both his arms around her waist and torso and pulled her tightly to him.

The gesture knocked the wind from Dahlia's lungs as she felt her body melding easily against his. She clutched the front of Guy's T-shirt, her eyes lifting to his. His stare was intoxicating, and Dahlia could feel herself slipping into the depths of his gaze, losing every ounce of her sensibilities in the longing that washed over her. She suddenly felt as if a part of her soul was sliding home. The connection was so strong, so intense, that she gasped loudly; the shock of the moment made it difficult for her to breathe.

Without giving it a second thought, Dahlia wrapped her arms around Guy's neck. His mouth was only a fraction of an inch from hers, and in a swift, delicate motion Guy closed the gap to kiss her, capturing her mouth with determination as he pressed his closed lips against her closed lips. His touch was velvet, soft and gentle, the sweetest caress of skin against skin, and Dahlia instinctively knew that no other man could ever kiss her like that.

Guy was holding on to Dahlia as if his life depended on it. He couldn't remember the last time he'd felt this way about anybody. He wanted to claim her and protect her, and that sudden knowledge both frightened and excited him. He felt Dahlia loosen her grip on him, attempting to back away ever so slightly, but he wouldn't let her. He tightened his hold, crushing her mouth with his as he savored the sweet taste of her. As his lips danced over hers he felt her shudder with excitement.

Their rising passion was undeniable as their gentle kiss escalated to a full-blown, openmouthed, tongue-twisting, deep-soul kiss that had Dahlia quivering in her high heels. An eternity passed before they broke apart, both gasping for oxygen.

Guy pressed his cheek to hers, still holding tightly to her, not wanting to let go. He leaned down to whisper in her ear, "I missed you, Dahlia, and I apologize for not calling you like I promised. Call me when you get home, no matter what time it is, and we'll make plans to meet for breakfast in the morning so I can start to make up for being such a fool."

Dahlia nodded, unable to form the words to answer him. He smiled brightly, brushing his fingers against the line of her profile. He pressed a row of damp kisses along her jawline, then his fingers glided where his lips had just rested. "And, if you don't call me, I *will* call you," he added as he finally let her go.

He turned his attention back to Drake who was staring with an opened mouth. Guy extended his hand a second time, acutely aware of the man's shock. "Good to see you again, Drake," he said casually. "Enjoy the rest of your evening. And make sure you get my friend home safely, please."

As he slowly strolled back to his table, a big grin appeared across his face. His brothers were high-fiving each other, signifying like only family could.

"You don't see that every day," Kendrick said, pushing the send button on his cell phone. He had cleverly captured the entire moment in a video to share with their sisters.

Mason shook his head. "I guess our brother isn't worried about things getting messy anymore," he said.

Donovan laughed. "You're the one who told him to step out on faith, big brother."

Mason nodded. "That I did," he said with deep chuckle. "That I did."

Chapter 10

Dahlia paced the halls of her home much like she'd tossed and turned in her bed the night before. Unease plagued her like a virus that was hell-bent on making her life miserable. She'd gotten little sleep, consumed by thoughts of Guy and his touch. The kiss they'd shared the night before had far exceeded the light peck on the cheek he'd given her days earlier, and she was overwhelmed by her reaction to it all. The fact that he'd done it in such a public manner didn't help the situation.

It had been some time since Dahlia had felt a connection with a man like the one she was feeling with Guy Boudreaux. The overrated movie star who'd wined and dined her into notoriety had come close to being "the one," moving her spirit more than any other man before him. That movie star had helped put her on the front page of every magazine and tabloid across the nation, completely enamored with their very public image. He'd even reveled when the media had blended their two first names into a singular nickname.

Behind closed doors, though, he'd been unsupportive of her, even confrontational, and all because Dahlia hadn't been ready to take their relationship to the next level. Intimacy had been an issue for Dahlia. She had not been ready when he had expected her to be, and when she'd said no, asking him to give her time, he'd been unwilling. After one argument too many, Dahlia had washed her hands of him and moved on. Since then she had refused to let herself get too close to any of her romantic interests, not lingering in a relationship long enough for any man to think that she should be ready and willing on his command. And Dahlia's choice to "not linger" is how she'd earned a reputation for loving and leaving the men who'd come into her life.

But Dahlia hadn't loved any one of them enough to even fathom making love to them, and casual sex wasn't on her list of things to do. Waiting for the perfect partner to make love with, however, was. And not every man met Dahlia's definition of a "perfect partner." Dahlia didn't take giving up her goodies lightly, most especially since she would be giving them up for the very first time.

Her virginity had always been an issue for other people, most especially the men who she'd gotten to know well enough to tell. But once they knew, not one of them had been willing to wait for her. And now here she was, contemplating those same crossroads with

Guy, wanting more but still not yet ready to cross to the other side.

Guy. Thoughts of him flooded Dahlia's mind. After a brief conversation over the telephone she was anxious for Guy to get to her home. To get to her. And that surprised her. She moved to peer yet again out an open front window, wishing she had a better view of the street to see him coming.

When he'd called her earlier, the sun was just beginning to appear in the new morning sky, and he'd apologized for waking her. She hadn't wanted him to know that she'd already been awake, dressed and anxiously waiting to hear from him.

She was thoroughly annoyed that she was so distracted by thoughts of *any* man. Even more irritated that she was so enchanted with *Guy*.

Just as he'd promised, when she hadn't called him, Guy had called her, his call coming even before she'd reached her front door the previous night. At first their conversation had been sketchy at best, both self-conscious and uncomfortable. Then Guy had joked about the planning of their second date. When Dahlia had countered with her own teasing retort about him not knowing how to return a telephone call, the comfort of small talk and their playful bantering had come back to them easily. And now she was excited at the prospect of seeing him again.

As he maneuvered his way through the streets of Los Angeles, following the GPS directions to the address Dahlia had given him, Guy was becoming increasingly irritated as traffic stalled his progress. He'd risen early, determined not to be late for breakfast with Dahlia. Determined to make amends for having been thoughtless.

Dahlia had given him a hard time about not calling, and he'd had to admit that he was just being a man about the whole thing. And like most men, he didn't always do what a woman expected him to do. In fact, Guy hated to admit that he rarely did what was expected of him. But for reasons he couldn't begin to explain, Dahlia Morrow had him thinking about doing things a little differently. Dahlia had him considering a lot of things that he hadn't given any thought to before.

After Dahlia had left the restaurant, he and his brothers' conversation focused on the boldness of his kiss and Dahlia's reception to him being so forward. And despite the very public opinion of his playboy status, in that very moment Guy had given serious consideration to a relationship that would last longer than a minute.

He let out a deep sigh as he rounded the corner of San Ysidro Drive and then turned onto San Circle. As he approached the gated community, he couldn't help but be impressed by the Beverly Hills neighborhood, home to some of the entertainment industry's most gifted talents. After passing the security guard's interrogation, he was waved through, and a man pointed him in the direction of Dahlia's home.

Her Mediterranean-style house sat at the end of the cul-de-sac. Pulling into the home's driveway, Guy was in awe of the terrain. Stepping out of his car, he found himself walking through the yard, moving from the front to the rear, to take in the views. With its resort oasis feel, the immaculate landscape boasted private patios, vast grassy lawns, an ocean-blue pool, a romantic fire pit with built-in bench seating, a barbecue center and absolutely stunning views of the city lights and vistas.

He was standing on her rear patio when Dahlia slid the glass doors open and stepped outside, two cups of steaming coffee in hand. She passed a large mug in his direction, her eyes smiling as she welcomed him to her home.

"Good morning," Dahlia said softly.

Guy leaned in and pressed a light kiss to her cheek, his lips lingering lovingly. "Good morning. This is beautiful," he said, his gaze sweeping over the landscape before landing back on her smiling face. "Although not as beautiful as you," he added.

Dahlia laughed, a soft chuckle that radiated from deep within her stomach. "You're silver-tongued and we haven't even had breakfast yet. What is a girl to do?"

Guy lifted his eyebrows in jest. "Just let a man do his magic," he said playfully. "So, what's for breakfast?"

She laughed again. "Whatever you're cooking. I told you last night that I don't cook."

He shook his head. "A woman who doesn't cook. Lord, have mercy!" he exclaimed, smiling brightly.

Dahlia stood with her hands on her hips, the sexy stance giving Guy reason to pause. Her hourglass figure tapered down to a slim waist and tight, rounded rear end and full hips. Her casual attire, a terry crewneck sweatshirt and matching shorts, showed off what even Guy could not fail to notice, a perfect bustline and a superb pair of legs. With her well-toned thighs and strong dancer's calves it was clear that she took very good care of her body; every one of her curves was tight.

She was barefoot, her toenails painted a vibrant shade of pink. Her bare café au lait complexion was sun kissed, and she looked incredibly healthy and toned. Instead of her usual conservative updo, her luxurious hair cascaded over her shoulders, the lengthy, reddish-brown strands framing her delicate face nicely. Dahlia's casual look was a striking contrast to the fashion-forward styling he'd become accustomed to seeing her in.

In that moment all Guy really wanted to do was to hold her in his arms like he'd held her the night before, to feel her body pressed tightly to his. He suddenly imagined what it might be like to have her naked before him, her flesh dancing hot against his own. As the lust-filled image clouded his thoughts there was little he could do to stall his want for her—it seeped from his eyes like water from a faucet.

Dahlia became visibly nervous as he stood staring at her intently, raging desire glazing his stare. With her knees beginning to shake ever so slightly, she wrapped her arms tightly around her torso. She cut her own gaze away from his and turned to stare out over her lawn. "Well, now," she muttered beneath her breath.

Guy shook his head, attempting to remove the sensuous thoughts he was having about her from his mind. "Let me get the groceries out of the vehicle," he said, quickly heading back in the direction of his car.

Dahlia watched as he strode confidently away from her. The testosterone in the air was palpable, his masculine aura like a thick blanket that had been wrapped around her shoulders.

Minutes later the two stood in Dahlia's oversize kitchen as Guy explained the nuances of beating fresh eggs.

Dahlia laughed out loud. "Do you approach everything so methodically?" she asked.

He nodded. "One must be precise to achieve near perfection," he answered.

She smiled sweetly as Guy gestured for her to take the whisk he held out.

"You want to whip air into them so they'll fluff up when you cook them," he said as he leaned to peer into the oven, eyeing a pan of biscuits inside.

As Dahlia began to beat the bowl of breakfast ingredients Guy shook his head. "Not so rough!" he exclaimed, stalling her hand with his own.

Guy moved in behind her, his body so close to hers that Dahlia would have sworn that she could feel the outline of every sinewy muscle of his broad chest pressing against her back. She took a swift breath, overwhelmed by the sensation of his sudden touch. Her body reacted with a mind of its own, her nipples blooming full beneath her top, the hardened buds pressing tight against the lining of her undergarment.

Her reaction seemed to encourage him. Guy moved even closer against her, cradling his pelvis tight against her buttocks. He nuzzled his face into her hair before whispering into her ear, "It's always better when you take it slow and easy." His voice dropped to a low murmur. She suddenly felt him harden in his slacks.

The heat wafting between them was combustible, drawing the air from her chest. Heat raged from the center of her feminine core, igniting a flame between them. It was suddenly so intense that Dahlia would have sworn that she'd stopped breathing and gone straight to heaven.

Dropping the cooking utensil into the bowl, she spun around in his arms. His lips were bent in the faintest of smiles and Dahlia was suddenly consumed with having them, wanting to taste him again. She lifted her face to his and kissed his full mouth. Their lips touched softly at first, then their tongues, both battling for dominance. Guy encircled his tongue with hers, and Dahlia yielded, moaning gently at the sensation. She sighed with pleasure as his hands came to a rest around her waist, his fingers sliding around to her buttocks as he pulled her tight against him. There was no denying that she loved the feeling of his hands on her. His hands were firm and strong, yet soft and gentle.

The moment was interrupted as Dahlia's house phone rang sharply for attention. As quickly as she'd kissed him, she pulled away, gasping lightly for air. They locked gazes, both in awe of the sensations sweeping between them.

"You're burning my breakfast," Dahlia muttered as she moved to the other side of the room and reached to end the shrill ring echoing around the space. "Hello?"

Reaching for a pot holder, Guy pulled the biscuits from the oven, saving them from the trash bin by mere seconds. Taking a deep breath, he watched Dahlia while eavesdropping on her conversation. The delight that had previously painted her expression suddenly transformed into worry and anxiety, and it was apparent that something or someone had shifted her good mood drastically.

Dahlia dropped the receiver back onto the hook. Tossing him a quick look, she moved into her family room, grabbed the television remote and turned it on. Following behind her, Guy watched as she changed the channel, eagerly searching for something.

As Dahlia dropped the remote to the table the station's commercial came to an end, flashing the station's call sign across the screen. A much-beloved newscaster appeared on the monitor, promoting the morning's entertainment news flash. Both Guy's and Dahlia's eyes widened as they stood and watched images of them together flashing across the screen; the newscaster's narration filled the surround sound.

"In entertainment news, everyone is asking if Oscar darling Dahlia Morrow and actor Guy Boudreaux of the famed James Bond franchise are an item. There was no straight answer to be had from either's camp this morning, so for now paparazzi photos of the two in a steamy embrace at dinner last night will have to speak for themselves. Spokespersons for both had no comment, but we certainly didn't hear a *no* from anyone. The two have been spotted dining together more than once recently, and sources say this leading man may be starring in more than just Dahlia Morrow's next film."

The segment ended with a picture-perfect shot of Dahlia and Guy in the previous night's lip-lock. The cohost of the segment chimed in with her own cheeky assessment as she fanned herself with her hand.

The two TV personalities laughed. "We'll keep you posted. Up next, James Cameron takes a pass on directing the sequel to his blockbuster film, *The Miracle Codes!*"

Dahlia switched off the television as she sank into the cushions of her chenille sofa. Guy dropped down onto the seat beside her. Neither said a word as they sat staring into the blank television screen. Dahlia finally broke the silence.

"I'm sure this will all blow over in a day or so. But from this point forward we need to maintain a strictly professional relationship. I don't want anything to interfere with the production of my movie, and gossip about us will deter everyone from focusing on what's important, and that's *Passionate*."

Guy nodded his head slowly. He shifted forward in his seat, his elbows resting against his thighs, his hands cupped together in front of him. He shifted his gaze to meet hers. "Is that what you really want?" he asked.

Dahlia took a deep breath. "It's for the best."

"I don't agree," Guy said. "I really like you, Dahlia, and I would like for us to get to know each other better. I think you feel the same way, or at least when I kissed you I did." He dropped a gentle palm against her knee; his touch sent a shiver up her spine.

"I don't know if what you or I might want is relevant. I have a movie to make, and right now that takes precedence over everything else. Even what I might want or might be feeling. And while I'm trying to make my movie a success I don't need to be distracted because everyone else is focused on my personal life. So, from this point forward we will be nothing but professional with each other."

Guy continued nodding, saying nothing. His hand was still pressed against her bare knee, gently kneading and caressing her flesh. There was nothing casual about the gesture—his touch was deliberate. Dahlia felt herself becoming aroused beyond measure. The sensation electrified her but also made her very nervous.

Guy leaned toward her and spoke gently into her ear. "No," he said defiantly. He straightened his back, staring into her eyes.

His voice was quiet, his posture commanding, and Dahlia felt herself tense, something undeniably provocative about his breathy voice. "What do you mean 'no'?"

"I mean no. I mean I want you and you want me and I don't care what anyone thinks about it. I'm not going to let rumors or the press or your damn movie keep us from exploring just how far we can go. That's what I mean."

Dahlia shut her eyes tightly. She wanted to agree with him, but something inside was holding her back. Her eyes opened, and she shook her head hastily, needing to stall the wave of emotion flooding her spirit.

"You can take your hand off my leg now," she said, hoping she sounded forceful and convincing. Hoping he couldn't hear the wanting in her voice.

Guy gestured with his head. "I could," he said as he continued to tease her, caressing her skin gently. "But you don't want me to." He slowly massaged her muscle, sweeping his fingers across her kneecap and up toward her midthigh.

Dahlia was desperate to say something, anything, but couldn't. The words were lost to her. Her stomach was tied in knots, and she felt thrilled and petrified at the same time. Never before had she wanted any man's touch as much as she suddenly wanted Guy's.

As if he could read her mind Guy leaned over and kissed her, a soft, gentle glide of his lips over hers. Without a moment's hesitation Dahlia found herself returning the kiss, wanting more, her hunger for him rising as if she were a woman who was starved for affection. And she was. She leaned into him as his fingers gently stroked her neck and his other arm snaked around her waist, drawing her tightly to him. Pulling his mouth from hers he moved his cheek against her cheek, caressing her flesh. He pressed a damp kiss behind her ear, tightening the hold he had around her as he wrapped both his arms tightly around her torso.

"What we will do is take it slow," he said, his voice so suggestive that Dahlia could feel a tingle of energy run down her spine. "We'll take it slow and focus on the movie, but we are not going to let this opportunity bypass us. Not until we both decide that it isn't going to work out between us. Deal?"

Closing her eyes, Dahlia allowed herself to fall into his chest, easing into the warmth of his embrace. She couldn't begin to fathom how they were going to make anything between them work, but she had to admit that she wanted to try. Because Guy was making her feel like she had never felt before. She finally responded. "Fine," she whispered softly. "It's a deal."

The words brought a bright smile to Guy's face. Lifting himself from the sofa, he extended his hand in her direction, pulling her to her feet. "We still have to finish breakfast. I'll cook the eggs. You set the table," he commanded as he kissed her cheek one last time before heading back to the kitchen.

Dahlia stared after him. A state of confusion washed over her face as she tried to make sense of what was happening, tried to figure out when she'd relinquished control to the man who was puttering around in her kitchen. Unable to discern an answer that made sense to her, she hesitantly followed behind him.

Chapter 11

As Guy pulled into the studio lot he noted the name-plate that marked his parking spot and grinned broadly. The first day of filming for *Passionate* had come faster than he'd realized. Almost two whole months had passed since he and Dahlia had negotiated their relationship. Two whole months since his life, and hers, had changed, the duo giving new meaning to the word *slow.*

His grin widened. As agreed, the two had been taking things slow, building a beautiful friendship. Despite the occasional speed bump, they'd been having a lot of fun together. Their friendship was only challenged when they found themselves alone, his lips pressed to hers, his body wanting more and Dahlia seeming to want more, too. There had been many a moment when he had wanted to toss caution right out the door, rip her clothes away and ravage her sexy body. But each time the thought crossed his groin, Dahlia had held him at bay, drawing a line in the sand that she adamantly refused to cross.

On more than one occasion he'd left her in frustration, a rock-hard erection like steel in his pants, every one of his nerve endings on fire. But Guy respected her wishes, not pushing for anything that she'd not been willing to give freely. Unfortunately, Dahlia was adamant about them not taking their relationship to a place of no return. She was also overly concerned with the media making more of their situation than was necessary. Despite his protests that no one would know what they were doing behind closed doors, Dahlia remained steadfast in her convictions. And despite his own desires and frustrations, Guy was determined to give her whatever her heart desired, even if she didn't know what that was.

Guy felt right at home as he entered the studio. The stagehands were putting the final touches on the sets; teams of people bustled about. Guy saw Dahlia before she saw him, and he stood watching her as she bellowed out instructions, pointing everybody in the correct direction. She was impressive to watch, clearly in full and total control. It was an extremely sexy quality in a woman. As he thought about her, Guy felt his chest push forward with pride.

He'd stood staring for some time before he caught Dahlia's eye and she waved excitedly, rushing to his side. Guy hugged her warmly as she threw herself into his arms, her exuberance igniting his own.

"You're early!" she exclaimed, smiling brightly.

"I'm being professional," he said as he kissed her cheek.

"Well, your costar arrived just minutes before you did. She's already in hair and makeup. I'll walk you down and introduce you," she said.

Guy nodded as he trailed along beside her. "So do we know why our illustrious lead didn't make it to the table reads?" Guy questioned.

Dahlia shrugged. "I'm discovering that your leading lady is a little temperamental."

He rolled his eyes. "An actress with a diva attitude. Just what a movie needs!"

"She just requires a lot of attention. She likes to have her ego stroked. Tell her she looks great and she'll be like putty in your hands."

Guy laughed. "Do you really want another woman being putty in my hands?" he said as he pressed a warm palm against the center of her back.

Dahlia shook her head. "I'll make an exception for this woman as long as you both deliver on film."

With a raised brow, Guy nodded but said nothing, intuition telling him that the next few weeks with the film star would prove to be more of a challenge than he could ever begin to anticipate.

Zahara Ginolfi was a fountain of complaints when Dahlia and Guy entered the space that would serve as her trailer for the duration of the film. The stylist who'd been hired to work with her was visibly frazzled, not having expected to be inundated with a wealth of unhappy so early in the morning. And Zahara Ginolfi was clearly unhappy.

"It's a horrible color," Zahara whined. "I can't wear red. Red will wash out my complexion. You'll have to do better than that!" she exclaimed, snatching the dress from the other woman's hands and throwing it on the floor.

Dahlia shook her head as she reached down to pick the garment up. "You don't get a say in wardrobe," she intoned. "Maybe on our next film together but definitely not this one."

"Well, I should," Zahara pouted. She reached for a cigarette from the pack that rested on the makeup table and then pulled a box of matches from a nearby drawer.

Reaching out, Dahlia eased the tobacco stick from her fingers. "There's no smoking here. This is a smoke-free facility. Sorry."

Zahara rolled her eyes back into her head, throwing the box of matches to the floor. "Unbelievable!" she exclaimed loudly as she snatched the cigarette back. "Do you know who I am?"

Dahlia took a deep breath and ignored the woman's tantrum. She gestured in Guy's direction. "Zahara, I want to introduce you to—"

Before Dahlia could complete her sentence Zahara leaped from her seat, eagerly extending her hand toward Guy's. "Guy Boudreaux. What a pleasure! I'm so excited to be working with you."

Guy held her hand gently, his fingers caressing the palm. He then leaned down to press a light kiss to the back of it. "The pleasure is mine, Zahara. I have a good feeling about us," he said, his bright eyes staring into hers.

Zahara giggled softly. "We should have met sooner. I can't believe our paths haven't crossed before now."

"I agree. I was hoping to meet at the table reads. I'm sorry you missed them."

"I never do table reads. Too much rehearsal and you lose the freshness of a role. I like the spontaneity, most especially with a romantic lead." She took a step closer to Guy. "I can already sense that you and I have great chemistry. I assure you it will play so much better on camera if we don't overwork or force it."

Guy's smile was smug. "Well, I'm excited. Let's get to work then and see what kind of magic we can make together," he enthused.

Zahara grinned broadly. She suddenly remembered that Dahlia was standing between them, still holding out the red dress that she'd discarded. She took the dress from Dahlia's hands and held it up in front of her.

Guy's enigmatic smile was consuming. "Actually, I think red will look wonderful on you," he cooed. "But I'm sure you'll be stunning in anything you wear."

With a soft giggle, Zahara fluttered her eyelashes. "You're right. I can make anything look good. Even this old thing!" she chuckled, tossing a quick glance in Dahlia's direction.

"Well, we'll let you get ready," Dahlia said. "I'll see you on set in an hour or so."

Guy kissed the back of Zahara's hand once more. "See you soon, *Passionate*."

Zahara blushed excitedly, giggling at the attention as she gave Guy her best pageant-queen wave.

As the couple stepped back into the hallway, closing the dressing room door behind them, Guy shook his head. "You mean putty like that?" he said, leaning in Dahlia's direction.

She fell back against the wall, her breathing coming in short gasps as Guy hovered above her, his body teasing hers as he stood too close for comfort.

"They're waiting for you in wardrobe and makeup," Dahlia whispered, her eyes dancing from side to side as she looked to see if anyone was watching them. She pressed a palm to his chest and pushed him away from her. "And I need to get to work. Professional, remember?"

Guy smiled and moved closer. "Well, as soon as I'm finished shooting today and you're done doing your directing thing, I've made plans for us."

"What kind of plans?" Dahlia asked, clearly distracted by the nearness of him and the hand that was drawing small circles against her bare arm.

"Me and you plans," he answered. He kissed her forehead, his lips like warm pillows against her skin. He winked an eye as he stepped back, allowing a cool breeze to blow in between them.

Dahlia inhaled deeply, then let the warm air escape past her lips. "You are determined to make this difficult for me, aren't you?"

Guy laughed. "Why, Ms. Morrow, I don't know what you're talking about," he said as he moved toward the door with his name on it; a bright gold star gleamed for attention against the hard wood.

As he disappeared behind the closed door Dahlia stared in his direction. It was becoming increasingly difficult to resist Guy. Every ounce of her wanted to bare herself open to him. But it wasn't the time or place for that, and she wasn't sure she was ready to take their relationship to that level. She knew that she would eventually have to explain her reasons for holding back and make him understand her reservations. And she knew that that conversation with him would have to come sooner than later. Dahlia collected herself and headed down the hall in the opposite direction. She had a movie to make, and when all else failed her, she knew that she could always depend on the work that she loved most.

"Quiet on the set!" Dahlia shouted, pausing until the noise level dropped. "And action!" she cued, pointing an index finger toward Guy and Zahara.

Within minutes everyone in the room was lost in the scene playing out on set; Guy and Zahara fueled each other's creative energy. Dahlia felt herself gasp as Guy grabbed the other woman's arm and pulled her across the room, Zahara steadfast in her determination to resist his efforts. Watching him, Dahlia was struck by Guy's vulnerability, his ability to expose himself so unabashedly. His performance struck a chord deep in her spirit, and she found herself wanting to rush in and hold him, to take every ounce of his hurt away, even if it was just pretend.

Over the past few weeks she'd come to enjoy the

romantic candlelight dinners, strolls along the Venice canals and shopping on Ventura Boulevard with Guy. Guy Boudreaux had to be one of the most romantic men she'd ever spent time with. He lavished her with time and attention, and when they were together, everything around them seemed to disappear. And with each second that they shared, Dahlia realized she was falling head over heels in love with Guy Boudreaux.

His loud cries brought her back to the moment as his character pleaded for Passionate to come back to him, beseeching her not to break his heart. The scene was emotional and challenging, and despite Zahara's diva antics there was no denying her natural talents or the blatant chemistry between her and her leading man. Witnessing them play off of one another was dynamic, and Dahlia could only begin to imagine how it would read across the big screen. Her eyes moved from the camera's monitor to the performance in front of her, noting the tears that had risen in Guy's eyes. She gestured with her hand to her eyes and an astute cameraman zeroed in on Guy's face, the close-up shot magnifying every ounce of emotion he was invoking.

Silence filled the space, nothing ringing through the room but the soft echo of Guy Boudreaux's pleas and the harsh tone of Zahara's admonishments; both actors had delivered their lines with an air of perfection. Dahlia couldn't fathom a second, third or fourth take being as powerful or as moving. The two had nailed it with their first shot.

"Cut!" Dahlia yelled, her gaze shifting from the monitor to Guy's face as the crew erupted with applause. Her heart skipped a beat as she watched him take a deep breath, then a second, shaking himself out of character. Guy must've sensed her staring because he lifted his eyes to hers and smiled, tossing her a wink of his eye just as his makeup person rushed in to powder the perspiration from his face.

Dahlia swallowed hard as she looked away, color heating her cheeks. As she focused her attention elsewhere she didn't notice Zahara studying her, and him, intently.

Chapter 12

Dahlia would have gladly stayed late to work on her film, but Guy had insisted she lock the studio doors the minute they were done filming for the day. He'd teased her with promises of a surprise that would need her full and undivided attention. Unaccustomed to being ambushed by plans she'd not made for herself, Dahlia was intrigued by the secrecy and the prospect of being waylaid by a man as sexy and as imposing as Guy.

As she made her way down the studio's steps, headed in the direction of the parking lot, she saw that Guy was parked at the end of the ramp. He grinned widely from a brand-new Jaguar XK convertible; the top was down and the front black leather seats reclined. He was casually dressed and appeared comfortable, a far cry from the resolute personality who'd poured his heart and soul out in front of her cameras just hours earlier. His broad grin was contagious, and she began to smile from ear to ear, as well, before easing her way into the passenger seat of his car.

"Nice ride," Dahlia said merrily.

"I know," Guy said with a deep chuckle. "And thank you."

"So, where are we headed?"

Guy shrugged. "You needed a night out and I figured I'd give you one."

"What I need to be doing is working."

"You work too much! And you don't play nearly enough. I'm here to make sure you play more."

Dahlia shook her head. "I get the impression that you play way too much."

"Only *after* I get my work done."

"That remains to be seen," Dahlia said smugly. "You still haven't told me where we're going."

Guy laughed warmly. "Why don't you just sit back and relax and do this my way, please."

Dahlia thought about arguing with him, but she didn't. Instead, she shrugged her shoulders and settled down into the soft leather seats. She had to admit that it did feel good to sneak away for a brief moment, with nothing on her mind to contemplate but a good time with a great-looking guy. She reclined her seat a bit more, settled back, closed her eyes and allowed the breeze to blow gently through her hair.

Guy cut an eye in her direction, smiling as she feigned disinterest—the not knowing, the not being in control, was clearly eating away at her. She was beau-

tiful the way she pouted, pretending not to care. He
slid his hand against the dashboard and turned on the
radio. An old Alexander O'Neal classic filled the space,
the crooner seeming to sing a love song that had both
their names written all over it. Guy nodded his head
in time to the beat, glancing at her a second time. As
if sensing his thoughts, Dahlia opened her eyes to gaze
back at him.

"What?"

Guy shrugged, his smile shining brightly. "Nothing. What?"

Dahlia giggled, closing her eyes again. As she sat
there she couldn't help but think that it was a dangerous
game the two of them played, touching with their eyes,
avoiding the want that lingered like a thick cloud. Both
were fighting to resist the temptation between them.

"There's something I need to tell you," Dahlia said
suddenly, her eyes flying open.

"What's that?" Guy asked, a warm palm dropping
against her thigh. Her breath caught deep in her chest at
the heat of his touch. His fingers burned hot against the
flesh beneath her denim slacks as he kneaded her leg
gently. His touch was affectionate and caring, warming her spirit.

As she met his gaze she dropped her hand against
his, entwining their fingers tightly together. Guy lifted
his forearm, bringing the back of her hand to his lips,
and placed an easy kiss against her skin. Dahlia enjoyed
the sensations sweeping through her.

"I need to tell you…talk about…me…us…" she
stammered, searching for words that made sense to

her. Wanting to explain her reluctance to move their relationship where it seemed destined to go. Guy stalled her.

"Hold that thought. We're here," he said, excitement simmering in his tone.

Dahlia took in her surroundings, sitting up as she looked around. A large sign gleamed with fluorescent lights, the billboard for the Devil's Night Drive-In theater greeted them. Dahlia laughed out loud.

"The movies? Really?"

"Not just any movie, Dahlia. The *drive-in movies*," Guy exclaimed excitedly. "And it's a double feature."

Dahlia smiled. "And you thought I'd love coming to the drive-in movies because…?"

"Aren't you a filmmaker?"

She laughed.

"Do you know any filmmaker who doesn't like movies?"

"You've got a point. So what's playing?" she asked as Guy handed his prepaid tickets to the man at the gate, then maneuvered his car to the top of the two-story parking structure in downtown Los Angeles. As he searched out a parking space near the front of the twenty-four-foot-by-eighteen-foot projector screen, she noted the DJ spinning music near the concession stand.

Pulling into a prime spot, he adjusted the speaker so it hung from the car door. Seconds later, a carhop on Rollerblades skated over to take their order of hot dogs, popcorn, soda and a large box of candy.

When everything was delivered, Guy reached into

the backseat, and Dahlia noticed a small cooler for the first time.

"What'cha got there?" she questioned, swallowing a bite of her hot dog.

Guy winked as he pulled a bottle of champagne that had been cooling on ice to the front seat.

"You don't know nothin' about this," he said teasingly.

Dahlia laughed. "Champagne? With candy?"

"Champagne goes with everything," he said with a hearty laugh.

Dahlia shook her head, unable to contain her own laughter.

Two hours later, Dahlia was cuddled close against Guy's chest as Hitchcock's classic film *Psycho* came to an end. Guy had enjoyed teasing her as she'd watched most of the movie from behind her fingertips.

"You know I'm going to have to tell people about this," Guy said jokingly.

"I hate horror movies," Dahlia countered.

"But they're not real." He laughed.

"I still hate them," she said. She pulled the bottle of champagne from his hand and swigged the last drop. "I can't believe you drank the whole bottle."

"Me! You were the lush tonight."

"I am not a lush," Dahlia professed, turning slightly to rest the empty container back in the cooler. As she turned, her right breast grazed his arm. She blushed profusely and was suddenly reminded of the conversation they needed to be having.

Guy was acutely aware of the soft curve of flesh that

grazed his upper arm. If only she knew how much he wanted to wrap his fingers around the lush tissue and tease her nipples until they were hard candy. A surge of heat blazed through his groin. He shifted his body, fighting to stall the rise of nature.

Leaning forward, he pulled his arm from around her shoulders. "We should probably put the top up," he said as he pushed the appropriate buttons, moving the car's roof to ease back into place. After turning the key in the ignition, he rolled up the car's darkly tinted windows.

"I didn't realize how cool it's gotten," Dahlia said, anxious for conversation.

"Do you want me to turn the heat on?" he asked, moving his arm back around her shoulders.

She shook her head. "No, this is comfortable," she answered as she cuddled back against him.

A pregnant pause settled awkwardly around them until Guy broke the silence.

"Dahlia, you know how much I care for you, right?"

She nodded. "I care for you, too," she muttered. She gazed up at him, meeting his intense stare.

"I'm having a great time with you," he continued.

She nodded. "Tonight's been a great night."

Guy hesitated a second time, unable to find the words to say what he was thinking. *To hell with words,* he suddenly thought, thinking that he was feeling much more for Dahlia than he was willing to admit. He pulled her closer to him, leaning to kiss her lips.

Dahlia's response was restrained as she brushed her lips against his and then pulled away, looking nervously around the parking area.

"No one can see us," Guy said, reading her thoughts. "Not a soul can see inside the car. That's why I put the windows up."

"And here I was thinking you were being chivalrous, making sure I wasn't cold."

"I was being gallant. I was making sure I could kiss you without an audience," he said as he kissed her a second time, his lips dancing slowly against her mouth.

"I guess you forgot about the front window, huh?" Dahlia said sarcastically, pointing with her index finger.

Guy laughed. "Nope!" He reached into the backseat and lifted a portable car sunscreen into his hands. When he'd fumbled the cardboard contraption into place, their front view completely blocked, he turned his attention back to Dahlia. "I have everything covered!" he exclaimed as he pulled her back into his arms and resumed kissing her.

Lost in the embrace, Dahlia closed her eyes, giving in to the sensations, the champagne dulling her senses.

"We shouldn't," she started, her efforts to deny her desire futile.

"We're not," Guy muttered against her mouth, his tongue moving in sync with hers.

Dahlia was suddenly aware of his hands skating over her shoulders and down her back. She felt him tug at the sides of her blouse, pulling it out from inside her jeans. He slipped his large hands up under her top, running his thick fingers against her back. His fingers slipped upward, determined to unsnap the hooks on her bra. Guy couldn't help but wonder who would have invented such a torturous device, causing a man more pain than a woman. When the strap finally slipped apart, he let his fingers caress her bare back, his touch hot and intoxicating. Dahlia moved closer against him as he slipped his hand from beneath her blouse and began to unbutton its pearl buttons.

Dahlia grabbed his wrist, holding it lightly. She wanted to stall his eager search but couldn't move herself to tell him no. His fingers were intent on getting the buttons undone as he continued to kiss her hungrily. Once his mission was accomplished Dahlia knew that he would slide her blouse and bra from her body. And despite her sensibilities telling her to stop, Dahlia didn't want to.

She reached out and began to lift his T-shirt. Their lips parted and they separated only long enough for her to pull off his shirt. With her own buttons undone, Dahlia let him slip her blouse off, allowing it to fall to the floor beneath her feet. Her bra followed. They kissed again as Guy pulled her back to him, one hand moving his seat to a reclined position so that Dahlia fell across his chest, the softness of her breasts pressed against the lines of his hardness. She inhaled swiftly, unnerved by how wonderful it felt, skin against skin, heat sweeping between them.

Dahlia kissed her way across his cheek, slipping slightly downward to nibble on the side of his neck, over to his ear, sucking on the tender flesh. He sighed with approval as she kissed her way back across his neck, tilting his head back to make her access easier. She couldn't begin to believe how brazen her behavior was; her forwardness was completely out of character.

As she thought about it she was suddenly anxious, feeling vulnerable and exposed. Pulling back, Dahlia crossed her hands over her chest, shielding herself from view. Guy moved his head to signal no, and grabbed both of her wrists, placing both palms against his waist. He kissed her lips, a quick peck, and then nuzzled his face into her neck, his mouth moving downward. When his lips touched the top of her breasts, each kiss was followed by a lick, his tongue teasing the outer edges of one breast and then the other. His tongue worked in tight circles, bathing the sweet flesh as he worked his tongue slowly toward the dark chocolate nipple until he was just circling around the hard bud. A soft moan rose from Dahlia's throat as he suckled her gently. The moan increased in volume as he drew the hard nipple between his lips, drawing it in deeply as he used the tip of his tongue to rub against it.

Guy moved his head back, with his lips tightly enclosing her flesh until it was pulled free and popped out of his mouth. He switched back over to her other breast, taking that nipple deeply into his mouth. Dahlia's eyes were closed tight as she concentrated on the pleasure sweeping through her.

Dahlia couldn't begin to fathom how she'd gotten into the position of lying on her back, the leather seat reclined until it was completely prone. Guy was propped above her as he continued to suck and then lick each hard nipple. He then slid into the seat with her, easing his body against hers and dropping his hands down to the waistband of her jeans as he worked to get the garment undone. She called his name, hesitancy ringing in her tone. "Guy, please…"

Guy hummed against her flesh. "Shh! It's okay," he said, his tone patient and soothing. Dahlia's gaze moved to the silver cover that blocked her view of the movie screen and the movie that was playing in the background. Soft music oozed from the speakers; nothing else was discernible. She drew her hands across the back of his head, her fingertips grazing his soft dreads. She closed her eyes, and waves of pleasure began to heat every nerve ending.

"I can't…" Dahlia whispered softly.

"Just let me touch you, please," Guy begged as he slipped his fingers into the opening of her pants and let them lightly slip over her silk panties. He moved his mouth back to her mouth and kissed her feverishly.

Dahlia grabbed his hand, stalling his search. It took every ounce of her fortitude to resist the impulse to throw caution to the wind and give in to his seduction. She grabbed his hand and pushed hard against his chest, drawing her knee up between them. Both were gasping heavily as Guy slid back over the center console and fell back into his own seat, one hand cupping the bulge that had bloomed hard between his legs. He swiped his other hand across his face, removing the rise of sweat that beaded his brow. Dahlia took a deep breath and then a second as she snatched her clothes from the car floor, fighting to get back into her bra.

"I'm sorry," Guy said suddenly, brushing a hand over his bare chest. "I don't know what I was thinking."

She shook her head as she rebuttoned her blouse. Her

voice came in a hushed whisper, her cheeks burning red from embarrassment. "You don't have to apologize. We both got carried away."

He reached for her hand and held it, squeezing her fingers tightly between his own. "I just…" He stopped, meeting her stare. "I want to make love to you, Dahlia. And I think you want to make love to me, too. But it shouldn't happen like this. You deserve better than the front seat of my car."

"Even if it is a luxury Jaguar?" Dahlia said teasingly, desperate to ease the rise of tension between the two of them.

Guy laughed. He leaned back over to kiss her cheek. "Baby, you don't deserve anything *but* the very best! The next time I'll drive the Rolls."

Chapter 13

Like a love-struck puppy Zahara eyed Guy with eager anticipation. They'd had a full week on set together and it seemed obvious to everyone except Guy that Zahara was quite smitten. Even Dahlia had taken note of the woman's obvious interest in him.

Since their encounter at the movies there had been an awkward tension between them. Dahlia purposely avoided Guy if it didn't have anything to do with the film. And the film had been as good an excuse as any to keep him at bay. Dahlia acted as though she was too busy with business to entertain the prospect of any kind of a good time.

Guy hadn't pushed, confused about what was happening between the two of them. But he missed her and the easy time they enjoyed sharing with each other, and with nothing else on his mind but Dahlia, he wasn't paying the likes of Zahara Ginolfi an ounce of attention.

As she eased her way to Guy's side, he couldn't help but think that she was becoming a bit of a nuisance.

"So, what's on your mind?" Zahara questioned, one hand brushing against his chest as she looped her other through his arm. "I've been trying to get your attention for ten minutes now and you've been ignoring me."

Guy smiled sweetly. "Sorry about that. I wasn't trying to be rude. I just have a lot on my mind."

"So, I see. Anything a girl can help you out with?" She flipped her dark locks over her shoulder.

Guy pulled his arm from hers, pretending to stretch his body. He crossed both arms back over his chest, locking his palms beneath his underarms. "No, thanks, but I appreciate your concern, Zahara."

She took a step closer to him, pressing her body close to his. "It's the least a girl can do," she said as she peered up into his eyes. "I was thinking," she continuted coyly, her voice dropping an octave. "I was thinking that it would be good for the movie if you and I were spotted out together. Some free publicity for the film. Fuel the headlines, so to speak." She gyrated her pelvis against his. "We could make it fun while we're at it," she whispered.

Guy felt his manhood twitch ever so slightly at her touch, then falter like a flame beneath a cold breeze. She blew warm breath into his face as she wrapped her arms around his neck. "It could be a *lot* of fun," she said with a raised eyebrow, apparently noticing his hesitation.

Guy took a step back as he pulled her arms from his neck. He continued to smile sweetly. "You're bad, woman! But I can't do that," he said.

"Why?"

"Because I'm in a relationship," he said, the words flying out of his mouth before he could catch them.

Zahara eyed him suspiciously. "With who? I was told you're not dating anyone."

Guy shrugged. It was on the tip of his tongue to call Dahlia's name, but he instinctively knew that to do so would put a wedge between them that he didn't need to go up against. He couldn't call Dahlia's name until Dahlia was ready for their relationship to be public. And Dahlia certainly wasn't ready because they hadn't yet defined what their relationship was. He suddenly realized that there was much the two of them needed to discuss, and soon.

"No one you know," he said aloud, the little white lie rolling off his tongue.

Zahara reached for her requisite cigarette, holding it between her fingers. "Is she in the business?"

Guy smiled. "You ask a lot of questions."

"You're not gay, are you?" Zahara asked, her eyes narrowing as she tapped the cigarette in the center of her palm. "She's not a he, is she?"

He rolled his eyes, ignoring her question.

"So why won't you tell me who she is?"

"She's someone very special, and we'd like to keep our personal life personal."

"Well, if you're off the market I know a few women

who are going to be completely heartbroken," Zahara mused.

"I hardly think so," he said, chuckling softly.

Zahara pressed her thin frame against him one last time. "I know so," she said, her voice dropping deeply. "But if you change your mind, I'm always available," she concluded too eagerly.

Guy nodded, winking his eye as he eased himself away from the woman. "I'll keep that in mind," he said, still laughing.

"Do you have a light?" Zahara asked, gesturing with the unlit cigarette she'd been holding on to.

He shook his head. "Woman, you know you can't smoke in here."

Across the room Dahlia eyed the two of them curiously. Just like a man, Guy seemed to be enamored with the attention that Zahara was tossing in his direction. So much so that Dahlia suddenly found herself bristling with jealous indignation. She took a deep breath as Zahara kissed his cheek then eased out of the room.

She paused, standing like stone in order to not to draw his attention. She watched as Guy looked around the space to see if anyone might have been watching before turning his attention back to his cell phone. Dahlia was suddenly reflective, thinking that maybe she'd been right to hold off taking their relationship to the next level.

They'd made plans to talk over dinner, and Dahlia was eager to welcome Guy into her home. But Guy looked frustrated as Dahlia opened her front door to greet him. As he eased inside, frustration gave way to irritation and discord washed over his face. His cell phone was pressed to his ear, tucked between his head and his shoulder as he maneuvered an armful of grocery bags.

Dahlia's moved to help him with his packages, curiosity painting her expression as she eavesdropped on his conversation.

"Really," Guy said unenthusiastically. "I appreciate the invitation. I really do, but I just can't make it tonight." He stopped talking to listen, his eyes rolling around and around as he took in what was being said to him. "Maybe another time," he offered.

After dropping the bags against the granite counters he leaned in to kiss Dahlia's cheek, his eyes still widened in annoyance as he continued to navigate his phone call.

"I really have to go, but again, I appreciate you calling." Guy paused to listen. He let out an exasperated sigh. "That's my other line, Zahara. I will talk to you later," he said as he finally disconnected the call.

He then slid his phone across the counter and tossed his hands up in exasperation. "Sheesh! That woman is persistent."

Dahlia laughed. "Zahara giving you a hard time?"

"I could take a hard time. What I can't take is pushy and aggressive. Today alone I had to tell her no a half-dozen times, and she still isn't taking the hint."

"What did she want?"

"To meet for dinner. I told her that tonight wasn't a good night. And I had to tell her more than once."

"I warned you that Zahara can be eager when she wants something. It looks like she wants you."

"Well, I don't have anything for her."

"You sure about that?"

Guy eyed her curiously, noting a hint of something he didn't recognize in her voice. "Are you jealous, Ms. Morrow?"

"No, of course not," Dahlia answered, shifting her gaze from his.

Guy leaned against the counter, his arms crossing over his chest. "You sound jealous."

Dahlia rolled her eyes, refusing to acknowledge the emotion that had painted her spirit. Despite Guy being able to read her like a book, she refused to give him the satisfaction of knowing that his flirtatious nature was an issue for her.

Guy laughed, pulling her into his arms. He kissed her cheek warmly. "My baby is jealous!" he teased.

Dahlia laughed again. "Be nice. I can't afford for you and my leading lady to fall out with each other."

"What you can't afford is for your man to be more interested in dining with an obnoxious superstar than cooking a five-course meal for you."

"Five courses?"

"Give or take two or three," Guy said.

"Hmm. That sounds exciting. So, what are you cooking?"

"Spaghetti."

Dahlia shook her head. "That's more like give or take four courses."

"I was going to make dessert, too," Guy said, a wide smile filling his face.

"You're funny!"

He leaned to kiss her again, his lips touching hers gently. "That's why you and I get along so well. You have a sense of humor."

"Well, I have some work I need to do. I'll be in my office."

"You're not going to help me cook dinner?"

"Nope!"

Guy leaned back against the counter, his arms crossed over his chest. "That's another reason why you like me. You'd starve if I wasn't around."

"No, I wouldn't," Dahlia said as she moved toward the door.

Guy tossed up his hands one last time. "Humor me, woman! Don't you know how to stroke a man's ego?"

As she moved out of the space, Dahlia laughed heartily and Guy laughed with her.

An hour later or so, he called Dahlia's name as he put the finishing touches on her dining room table, setting two places for their evening meal. When Dahlia didn't answer, he headed toward the other end of the house.

Inside her office Dahlia was reclined against the chenille sofa, her legs resting on a cushioned ottoman. Her head was tossed back against a plush pillow, her mouth opened slightly as she snored softly. The papers she'd been reviewing had slipped to the floor, and from what Guy could ascertain she'd probably fallen asleep within minutes of sitting down.

Easing into the room he took the seat beside her,

perching himself on the edge of the sofa. He pulled at the lacings that tied her Grecian sandals, then eased them off her feet. He smiled as she snuggled down into the cushions, stretching and curling her pedicured toes. She purred softly and then muttered under her breath, "Thank you. That feels goods."

"Glad to be of service. How tired are you?"

Dahlia took a deep breath. "Very. But I didn't mean to fall asleep."

"I'm sorry I woke you. You need to rest better," Guy intoned.

"I have too much to do. I'll rest when it all gets done."

Guy moved to the other end of the small sofa as he guided her legs onto the cushions. He rested her feet in his lap and began to massage the soles, his thumb and forefinger deliberately pressing the stress and tension from her body. Dahlia's eyes were still closed, but her head swayed slightly with pleasure.

Guy cleared his throat. "This afternoon I told Zahara that I couldn't go out with her because I was in a relationship," he said, cutting his eye toward Dahlia as he waited for her reaction.

He felt her tense up, the muscles tightening through her calves. He continued, still kneading and stroking her limbs gently. "I didn't mention your name, Dahlia, but I wanted to. I wanted her to know that you and I are in a relationship. I want everyone to know how I feel about you."

Her eyes still closed, Dahlia took a deep breath, her chest rising and falling. There was a moment of awkward silence as Guy waited for her to acknowledge his comment. Dahlia could feel him staring, sensed him eyeing her intently. She opened her eyes to meet his gaze, staring just as attentively.

"How do you feel about me?" Dahlia asked, her voice a low whisper.

Guy paused, his eyes skating from hers. "I…well… I…" he stammered nervously then broke out into a sheepish grin.

Nodding her head, Dahlia smiled. "I haven't had a lot of success with relationships, Guy. I'm sure you've heard."

"You were never in a relationship with me."

"So that's the secret to success…being with you?"

"I think so."

Her own grin was a mile wide as she nodded her head. "And you want to go public with our relationship?"

"I don't want to hide the fact that we are making a commitment to each other. I want everyone to know that you are officially off the market, completely devoted to me and happy," Guy said.

He made Dahlia laugh, and the hearty sound pleasantly filled the room. "That works both ways, I hope."

"Of course. I want people to know I'm happy, too."

"And off the market!"

"I don't know about all that now," Guy said teasingly.

Dahlia laughed again. "I do. You are officially off the market, Guy Boudreaux."

Guy grinned widely. "Thank you, *Gahlia!*"

Dahlia groaned. "The media is going to have a field day with that one," she said.

"Wait until we have that baby! That's really going to send them over the edge."

"What baby?" Dahlia asked, her eyes narrowing sharply.

Guy went back to caressing her feet and toes, ignoring her question.

"What baby?" she asked a second time.

Guy laughed. "We don't have to worry about it until after the wedding, of course, but every celebrity couple has a baby. We, of course, will have the celebrity baby of all babies! Think how cute the little thing is going to be!"

"But it would be a little baby, not a little thing, Guy." A warm smile filled her face. "You are so crazy," she said.

"Let me take care of that, please. I've got the baby thing under control."

"Except that I would be the one who would have to get pregnant, remember?"

Guy laughed. "A technicality." He suddenly turned serious. "Have you ever thought about having kids, Dahlia? I mean, is that something you would want to do at some point? Be a wife and mother? And in that order 'cause my mother would have a fit if we did it any other way."

She paused, staring off at a spot behind his head as she pondered his question. She had thought about a family and a future with a man who'd be the father to her children. And she'd thought about it more since meeting Guy than she had ever before. The sudden realization that she wanted it more than she could have ever imagined swept over her spirit. It was in that moment that Dahlia knew beyond any doubts that nothing was ever going to be the same for the two of them again.

"Dahlia?" Guy caressed her gently, anxiously awaiting her response.

She turned her gaze back to meet his, a sweet bend to her mouth warming her expression. As she nodded her head, Dahlia's smile brightened. "Yes, I have thought about it, Guy. And, yes, I do want to have kids some day and be a wife and mother." She paused again. "But there's one more thing…." She paused. "I only want those things with you, Guy Boudreaux."

Guy swiped a hand across his brow. "Whew! You had me nervous for a minute, woman."

Laughing, Dahlia leaned back and closed her eyes, wiggling her toes beneath his palms. Guy resumed his massage, determined to ease every ounce of tension from her body. Dahlia reveled in the sensations.

"Oh, that feels so good," she moaned.

Guy chuckled under his breath as he continued his ministrations, his attention focused on each individual toe, then the arch, the instep, the sole, the heel. He was slow and methodic, his touch outrageously delicious as currents of pleasure shot from the tip of her toes to the top of her head.

The sensuous feeling was suddenly distracting, and Dahlia opened her eyes to stare at him, trembling from the arousal he was inciting. She felt herself tremble with pleasure.

"We should go eat," she said, pulling her limbs from his touch. "You are probably burning my spaghetti."

Guy bristled slightly. "Why do you do that?"

"Do what?"

"Pull away from me when it starts to feel good to you. Why don't you like me to touch you, Dahlia?"

Dahlia took a deep breath. "Because when you touch me, Guy, it feels too, too good. Too good to be right for anyone," she said matter-of-factly.

"It's supposed to feel good, Dahlia. It should feel so good that all you want is more."

"More isn't always a good idea."

"Says you." Guy shifted her legs back to the floor as he moved his body closer to hers. He wrapped his arms around her torso. "I think more is definitely a good idea." He nuzzled his face into her neck. He murmured his words against her skin. "I want more, Dahlia. I want more of you. But you have to want it, too."

Dahlia closed her eyes as she leaned into the path of the damp kisses he trailed across her jawline. He paused to suckle the spot beneath her chin. So lost in the sensations, Dahlia stuttered, her thoughts a mush of incoherent words. "I…don't… I…never… We…shouldn't…"

Guy moved from her neck to her lips and kissed her hungrily, the weight of his body pushing her back against the sofa as he eased his body above hers. He stalled her words as he kissed her mouth, his tongue eagerly searching for her consent.

Without giving it a thought, Dahlia wrapped her arms around his waist, clasping her hands together at the curve of his buttocks. She felt her legs fall open and

Guy drop himself between them. She felt the rigidness of his erection pressing through her clothes, resting just below her stomach; the resulting sensations swept like a firestorm through her.

Dahlia muttered again, her palms against his broad chest. "Guy…I…" she started, but then she was too breathless to even think straight. She suddenly didn't want to resist anymore; her wanting Guy was consuming. She wrapped her arms tightly around his torso and pulled him closer.

Guy continued to kiss her mouth, his tongue eagerly searching hers. Nothing about her body had been in agreement with the words coming from her mouth. Everything about Dahlia's body language was saying that she wanted him as much as he wanted her. And he wanted her, so much so that he imagined that if she told him no, he would explode from the frustration.

But he knew that if she did resist, and if she did tell him no, he would readily comply. Their being together wouldn't mean anything if Dahlia didn't want it as much as he did. He also knew that it would take every ounce of fortitude within him if it became necessary to stop.

As she curved her body against his, his blood surged, and Dahlia seemed to follow where he intended to lead her. His hands glided with ease across her lower back and onto her bottom; she didn't resist her legs wrapping around his waist. She purred softly, the sound like a sweet melody to his ears. He moaned in response, whispering her name into her hair. He suddenly needed to be free of his clothes, and hers. All he was focused on was wanting to bring Dahlia nothing but pleasure.

Chapter 14

Moving to his feet, Guy slowly pulled his black silk T-shirt over his head and tossed it to the floor. His hands grazed his broad chest and her eyes followed as he slid them to his waistband. In an impromptu striptease, he undid his belt buckle, unsnapped his jeans and lowered the zipper, all the while gyrating his hips in a slow, erotic rotation. As he stepped out of his leather loafers, his eyes were locked on Dahlia, who was eyeing him feverishly. She gasped loudly as he pushed his jeans and boxers to the floor, stepping out of the garments as he kicked them aside, standing naked before her. Dahlia's eyes widened in wonder. Her gaze skated over the lines of his tight chest and stomach muscles, down to the rigid, well-proportioned length of manhood that was pointed straight in her direction.

Having never seen a man so up close and personal before, Dahlia's eyes took in his entire body. Then her stare locked on the length and fullness of the dark chocolate marvel. Everything about the man was intoxicatingly beautiful and unnerving. A wry smile filled Guy's face as his hand clamped between his legs. He met her intense stare as he boldly stroked himself.

Her breath catching in her chest, Dahlia's face flushed a deep, dark shade of crimson red. Overwhelmed, she suddenly bolted from her seat, almost racing to the office door. Guy quickly called after her in surprise.

"Dahlia, baby, what's wrong?"

Pausing in the entranceway Dahlia bit down against her bottom lip. Her knees were shaking so much that she couldn't grasp how she was still able to stand. Her eyes misted with salty tears. "Let's take this to the bedroom," she said, turning abruptly.

With his hands on his hips Guy stared after her curiously. He sensed that something about the moment was off-kilter and it shouldn't have been. Maybe Dahlia wasn't feeling him the same way he was feeling her. He couldn't help but think that maybe he'd misread her cues. Taking a deep breath, he cupped his palm between his legs, stalling the wave of heat that had washed over his loins. He reached for his pants, lifting them from the floor. Just as he moved to step back into them he heard Dahlia calling his name. Calling him to her. He took another deep breath.

"Guy? Are you coming?" Dahlia called again.

Then, Guy reconsidered, maybe he had read her cues

just right. Tossing his pants back to the floor, he exited the space, racing to catch up with the woman, his naked frame eager for her attention.

Inside her bedroom Dahlia stood in front of a large, ornate mirror with a lavish gold frame. She stared at her reflection, her hands clutching her shirt beneath her chin. The room was large, beautifully decorated and dimly lit.

Moving behind her, Guy dropped his palms to her shoulders, then moved them down her sides. He pressed a kiss to the back of her head as he wrapped her in a deep embrace, pulling her against his chest.

"Are you okay?" he asked, concern flooding his tone. "I mean…if you don't want this…" He paused.

The edges of Dahlia's mouth eased into a slight smile. "I'm just nervous," she whispered. "Doesn't the first time with someone make you nervous?"

"I'm excited," he said softly. "I'm excited for us to be intimate with each other. I'm excited about wanting to make love to you."

Dahlia's smiled widened slightly. She closed her eyes in an attempt to halt the wave of anxiety that was threatening to consume her. As she did Guy blew kisses against her neck and shoulders. She opened her eyes to stare at the reflection of the two of them together.

"Put your arms up," he said softly, meeting her gaze in the reflection.

After taking another deep breath, Dahlia did as she was told. Guy reached around her and undid the loose knot that held her top in place. He guided it off her shoulders and dropped it to the floor. Moving closer against her, he put his arms around her waist and rested his hands on her stomach. He continued to eye her in the mirror as he kissed her neck and whispered in her ear.

"You are so beautiful," he said softly. "I'm going to take all your clothes off. I want to see you nude."

Dahlia nodded, still staring at him in the mirror.

Guy slid his hands up her stomach and under her bra cups. Then he pulled it up and over her head instead of unsnapping it from behind. He smiled as he watched her watching him. His fingers found her nipples, and she watched him play with her, rubbing his palms against the lush tissue, then pinching and rolling the nubs between his fingers. He traced his nails lightly around her breasts.

"These are gorgeous," he whispered as he grasped two handfuls firmly in both palms, juggling them like melons being weighed. It made Dahlia smile, and Guy smiled with her.

Dahlia could feel her excitement rising, dampness beginning to puddle between her legs. Guy nibbled the back of her neck, kissing her shoulders as he continued to play with her nipples.

"My girl likes this, doesn't she?" he whispered, his breathy tone searing.

Dahlia moaned. "Yes... Oh, yes," she said, her head falling back against his chest, her eyes open wide.

"Will you do anything I ask, Dahlia? Will you?"

Dahlia moaned again. "Yes...anything..."

Guy moved around in front of her, his hands never leaving her body. He pulled her tight against him, her bare breasts kissing his chest. He leaned in to kiss her, his hands sliding to the back of her head, and he pulled her into him. The kiss was soft and gentle, increasing in urgency. Dahlia wrapped her arms around his torso, hugging him tightly as she pushed her tongue past his lips. She kissed him intensely, her hands dropping to the curve of his buttocks.

Guy suddenly swept her off her feet, lifting her into his arms. He moved to the bed, snatching the bedclothes away with one hand before lowering her to the sheet-covered mattress. Standing above her, he pulled at her shorts, then her bikini-cut panties, pulling them both down to her ankles and off with ease. Seeing her lying splayed before him, Guy couldn't imagine himself loving any other woman as much as he knew that he loved Dahlia. His heartbeat quickened, beating like a steel drum in his chest. His manhood throbbed, protruding from his body with a need that was indomitable. It was almost too much for Guy to bear. He fought to keep himself from exploding.

More exposed than ever before, Dahlia couldn't begin to imagine the pleasure getting any better. Everything about Guy's touch had her convulsing. No man had ever gotten her to the point of no return, and she sensed that Guy was about to take her right over the edge.

Hovering over her, he kissed her mouth. She kissed him back, harder, the passion rising with a vengeance between them. Guy pressed his tongue against her lips and they parted slowly, welcoming him in. He felt himself throb at the sensation.

Dahlia clasped her hands around his bottom and

pulled him hard against her. He felt the bump of her mound pressing against him. He felt himself harden even more, the sweetness of it almost painful.

Guy slowly kissed his way down to her neck. He continued a slow crawl down her body, his lips pressing damp kisses over her breasts, across the tight abdominal muscles, pausing to lick the core of her belly button. Dahlia's body tensed slightly at the prospect of where his leisurely stroll was about to take him. She pressed her knees tightly together, stalling the wave of heat that felt like a volcanic eruption between her thighs. Guy gripped her by the hips and pulled her toward him until her center was inches from his face.

He smiled up at her, winking an eye. "Don't look so nervous. This is my favorite part!"

Dahlia gasped loudly, words catching deep in her throat. She could only imagine the expression on her face, picturing herself looking like a deer caught in headlights.

Guy slid his hand down and back up the sides of her legs, his fingers tickling the backs of her knees. His hands caressed her bare behind, and then he pressed his mouth against her slit, kissing her intimately. Dahlia felt as if she'd stopped breathing; the sensations were so intense. Her hands dropped against the back of his head as he nibbled her labia, flicked his tongue against her clit and pressed his tongue deeply into her. Dahlia could feel how wet she was, moisture dripping from her center. Never before had she felt anything so consuming. Not one of her favorite romance novels had prepared her for the intense sensations sweeping through her body.

Pushing and pulling at her legs, Guy licked and tongued her, murmuring and whispering sweet, dirty things against her secret box. Every time Dahlia felt herself about to explode he stopped, his gaze lifting to meet hers. She had never been so turned on. It was too much, and when Dahlia felt herself completely at the edge, ready to free-fall into ecstasy, Guy pressed his hand firmly against her core, somehow stopping her orgasm.

"Don't move," he commanded as her hips moved involuntarily, lifting to meet his palm. He stood up and reached for a condom he'd placed on the nightstand. After tearing at the wrapper with his teeth, he sheathed himself quickly.

Dahlia bit down against her bottom lip, staring at him intently. With her legs spread so unabashedly, she suddenly felt vulnerable and began to slowly close her knees.

Guy shook his head, both of his hands pressing against the insides of her thighs. "I said don't move. I want to see you. Don't close your legs to me," he commanded a second time.

Dahlia took a deep breath and held it, allowing her legs to fall open as Guy stared down at her. He dropped back between her thighs, kissing up the inside of one and then the other. He parted her with his fingers, his tongue wildly flicking her clitoris a second time as his tongue trailed through the silky hair. Her juices flowed like water from a faucet. Dahlia moaned loudly. "Oh, yes, oh, oh, yes." She was suddenly clutching her hands to her chest.

Her orgasm was crushing as she seemed to come again and again and again. Her hips flexed forward and her bottom clenched tightly. Guy did not let up, continuing to lick her private place until she was spent, quivering from the convulsions.

Gasping for breath, Dahlia opened her eyes as Guy lifted her legs, bending her knees back toward the mattress as he lifted her hips and buttocks off the bed. He pulled her closer, crawling on his knees until his own pelvis was pressed tightly against her. Dahlia felt herself tense as Guy pressed himself against her garden door, the length of him tapping for admittance.

Pushing forward, he penetrated the virginal cavity, his body falling against hers as he braced himself on his forearms. There was a brief moment of resistance that gave him pause, and Guy suddenly stopped in midstroke.

Concern cracked his voice as he called her name. "Dahlia?"

He was staring at her intently, confusion washing over his expression. Shaking her head, Dahlia wrapped her arms tightly around his torso. She took a deep breath and held it, then lifted her hips upward to meet him. The motion was swift and the sharp pain was over with before she could so much as blink. She suddenly felt warm and full as her warm breath escaped past her lips.

Guy lay cradled deep inside her, his body tight to hers. Understanding suddenly swept through his spirit; the knowledge that this was her first time and he was truly her first was almost too much for him to absorb.

Tears misted her eyes, and he gently wiped at the moisture with the backs of his fingers.

"Why didn't you tell me?" he whispered as he drew his hands through the length of her hair, his mouth pressed against her ear.

She shook her head a second time. "It's not important. Just make love to me," Dahlia whispered back, breathing heavily.

Guy hugged her tightly, melding his body tightly against hers. His first strokes were long and slow and he watched as she shivered with each one, her face contorting with pleasure at the gentle friction of flesh against flesh. Neither could imagine anything sweeter. Their lust was intense as Guy continued to push and pull at her slowly. His lips went back to the tasty flesh of her right breast and then the left, suckling her easily. Shifting back upward, he nuzzled his face against her neck. He heard the soft moan in her throat rising steadily until she was chanting his name over and over again.

With his own arousal increasing at a steady pace, rising with a mind of its own, Guy's strokes increased, the rhythmic push and pull of his body inside hers augmented by its own beat. The two danced together like no two before them, the connection intoxicating. She was velvet around his steel, silk stroking his rigid hardness. He felt her tremors, convulsive ripples that gripped him hard. Then Dahlia screamed out loud, Guy's name spinning off her tongue. She clutched him tightly, unable to imagine them any closer or anything so intimate being so extraordinarily beautiful, and then they exploded simultaneously. Dahlia's eruption had triggered Guy's.

An eternity passed as Dahlia lay panting heavily beneath him. Guy struggled to catch his own breath, taking deep gulps of air as he waited for his heart to stop racing. He could feel her heartbeat tapping in time to his, and he would have given anything to have stayed there forever.

He finally rolled from above her, sprawling out across the empty space beside her. Her eyes were closed, her chest rising and falling rhythmically. Reaching for her hand, Guy entwined her fingers beneath his and held on tightly.

"Are you okay?" Guy asked softly, turning his head to stare at her.

Dahlia nodded, not meeting his gaze.

He leaned up on his elbow to stare down at her. "Don't do that, Dahlia," he said. "Talk to me, baby. I need to know that you aren't traumatized or something."

Dahlia laughed heartily. "Why would I be traumatized?" she asked, finally opening her eyes to his. "Are you doubting your skills, sir?"

"My skills aren't in question. You not telling me that you were a virgin is the issue on the table right now."

"Would it have made a difference? Would you not have made love to me?" She slid her body closer to his, curling up against him.

Guy shook his head. "I might have held off," he said.

"Really?"

"Well, we would have talked about it more, at least."

"We didn't need a whole lot of conversation, Guy."

"But we should have—" He stopped in midsentence as Dahlia pressed an index finger to his lips.

"We did exactly what we were supposed to do, Guy," she whispered.

He shook his head as he curled himself against her. "Yes," he said, his voice a loud whisper against the curve of her arm. "But I wouldn't have waited for the chance to tell you I love you, Dahlia. I would have told you that first."

Dahlia felt her tears rising again. "You can still tell me that now," she said, savoring the heat from his body.

Guy drew his fingers against her cheek. He pressed a tight kiss to her closed lips. "I do, you know. I love you, Dahlia Morrow."

Dahlia giggled softly as she met his gaze. "I love you, too, Guy Boudreaux, very much. Now, can we do it again?"

Chapter 15

Leslie eyed Dahlia curiously as the woman rushed into the office, her face flushed. She glanced up at the clock over her desk and shook her head.

"I know. I know," Dahlia said. "I'm late."

"What's up with you today? You are never late for anything."

Dahlia shrugged as she quickly flipped through a stack of papers, searching for the previous night's call sheets.

Leslie studied her intently. "And you're glowing! Really, what's up with you?"

Dahlia giggled. "Nothing. I just overslept is all."

Leslie nodded her head slowly. "You got some, didn't you?"

"What are you talking about?" Dahlia said, refusing to meet her friend's gaze. "I didn't get anything."

"Uh-huh, yes, you did. You got you some. Who kept you from getting out of bed this morning, Dahlia?"

Dahlia shook her head. "You're crazy, Leslie."

Leslie laughed. "And you're a bad liar."

Dahlia laughed with her, ignoring her admonishment. "I've got to get to the studio. I'll barely have time to go through yesterday's dailies before we have to start shooting."

Leslies glanced at the clock a second time. "You're fine. The crew had a five-thirty call time. Your cast has to report to wardrobe and makeup at ten. It's just seven. You have plenty of time. So, why don't you enjoy your coffee and tell me about your weekend."

Dahlia shook her head. "I don't have anything to tell," she said, reaching for the morning beverage Leslie held out to her.

"Sure you don't!" Her friend rolled her eyes. "Well, this might be of interest to you," she said, passing Dahlia a copy of the *New York Post,* the morning newspaper opened to the celebrity gossip on page six.

"What's this?" Dahlia asked, scanning the paper's byline. Her name jumped out at her as she read the few short lines of celebrity news. She shook her head repeatedly, unable to fathom how quickly gossip traveled from point A to point B. "And I wonder who the unnamed source could be?" she said, annoyance floating over her face.

"Well," Leslie said, interjecting her two cents, "I imagine that if it wasn't you and it wasn't Mr. Boudreaux, then maybe, just maybe, Zahara Ginolfi might have had something to do with it."

Dahlia's head still waved from side to side. "Unbelievable," she exclaimed.

"But I'm willing to put my money on Guy having been in your bed last night, and not Zahara's, despite the assertions that there is tension on the set because you're trying to steal her new man."

Dahlia blew out a deep sigh. "What is it they say?" Her eyebrows lifted. "Bad press is better than no press?"

"Girl, I don't know what you're talking about. This is some good press."

"You're stupid!" Dahlia laughed. "I've got to run. I've got a movie to make."

When she got to the door, Leslie called her name.

"What?"

"Was he good?"

Dahlia grinned. "Leave me alone, Leslie," she said as she moved out the door.

She could hear Leslie's laugh ringing behind her. "That's what I'm talking about. You go, girl!"

Guy reached for his cell phone, pulling it to his ear. "Hello?"

"Where are you?" his sister demanded through the receiver. "I'm here at your apartment and you aren't here. And I called and they said you haven't made it to set yet."

"Good morning to you, Maitlyn." He yawned as he stretched his body out across the bed. "I have another two hours before I have to be on set."

"Where are you, Guy?"

"In bed."

"Whose bed?"

"What's the matter, Maitlyn?"

"*The Morning Show* wants to interview you about your new film and your new relationship."

"What relationship?" he asked, his eyes opening wide.

"Well, if I believe any of the gossip, your new relationship with your costar Zahara. To hear her tell it you two are quite the item."

"Well, we're not."

"And that's why she's on *The Morning Show* telling the world that you are the lover in her life."

Guy rolled his eyes. "No, she's not."

"Yes, she is," Maitlyn screamed into the receiver. "Turn on your television!"

Guy sighed. "I can't. Dahlia doesn't have a television in her bedroom."

His sister laughed. "I am so telling Mommy!"

"Leave me alone, Mattie!"

Guy listened as his sister sighed over the receiver. As his agent and manager Maitlyn was responsible for every aspect of her brother's career. As his big sister she felt overwhelmingly responsible for his personal life, especially if he could learn a life lesson from her mistakes. If tossing two cents into his personal affairs gave him something to think about then it was well worth the expenditure, she had once told him.

"I'm getting questions from the media, Guy. What do you want me to say?"

"Say that I'm in a very good place in my life and that I'm very happy."

"And you're in this good place with Zahara?"

"Hell, no!" Guy said emphatically.

"With Dahlia?"

"Of course with Dahlia. Who else would it be?"

"You say that like it's something I should know."

"You should."

"And you've been keeping me up-to-date with your love life for how long now?"

"All of two minutes, so you should have no problems getting it right."

"You are going to drive me crazy, baby brother."

"I'm keeping you on your toes."

"A word of advice, little brother."

Guy shook his head. "Is this going to be a lecture? Because I don't have time for a lecture. I'm making time this morning."

"No, just something for you to think about. You obviously like Dahlia and she seems to like you, so you need to remember that because of your professions, your personal lives are bound to play out in the media for public scrutiny. And though most of it might be a fabrication, what they say about there being fire where there's smoke does have some truth to it. Zahara's clearly fanning flames about you and her for a reason. And true or not, I'm sure Dahlia, being a woman, can't help but wonder why. I know I would."

"So what are you trying to say, Mattie?"

"I'm saying that you need to be mindful that you aren't giving Zahara firewood to work with. I'm saying you need to get her in check and do whatever you have to do to douse those flames fast. Do it for Dahlia."

There was a brief moment of silence before Guy spoke again. "I'm going to take Dahlia with me to New Orleans this weekend to meet the old people. Are you going to be around?"

"I'm sure we will all be there for that," she answered.

Guy laughed. "Don't scare her, Mattie. She loves me."

His sister laughed with him. "And do you want me to tell the press that, too?"

"Yeah," he said softly. "And don't forget to tell them that I love her more."

Zahara's morning interviews made the front page of the evening tabloids. Despite Guy's assertions that nothing was going on between him and Zahara, and Dahlia knowing how the press loved to run with a good lie, she couldn't help but wonder if there might have been an inkling of truth to the story.

Zahara and Guy were amazing on-screen together. Rarely had Dahlia seen that kind of chemistry between actors who didn't have some kind of history between them. It was obvious that Zahara liked Guy. In fact, it was clear that she liked him a lot. And Guy did have a reputation for being quite the ladies' man. But then, so did she, Dahlia thought suddenly. To hear the media tell it, Dahlia had gone through men like some people changed their undergarments. And knowing the truth of her own situation, Dahlia knew Guy's, as well. And she knew that she had no reason whatsoever to doubt what was growing between them.

Dahlia knew that she was being foolish to doubt

Guy's feelings because she'd finally decided to take their relationship to the next level.

Always one to make an entrance, Zahara showed up an hour after her call time. Anticipating her late arrival, Dahlia was already filming another scene, oblivious to the woman's bad behavior.

As Dahlia directed the actors, in deep conversation with the cast about what she wanted, Guy sat on set watching her. He bristled as Zahara moved to his side, sliding her arm through his as she leaned in to kiss his cheek.

"Did you see my interview?" she whispered.

"What interview?" Guy whispered back.

"*The Morning Show.* I made sure we got some good press."

Guy shrugged, his gaze still focused on Dahlia. "Sorry, I missed it."

"I think we should do dinner tonight. We need to be seen out in public."

Guy sighed, cutting his eye in the woman's direction. "That's not going to happen, Zahara. Sorry."

"Why not?"

"I told you before. I'm in a relationship with someone. And I'm not interested in people thinking that you and I are in a relationship together."

"Dahlia's been around the block a few times. If I were you I wouldn't want my name linked romantically with hers. With her reputation you're just another notch on her very long belt."

Guy tensed, shaking the woman's grip from his arm. "Zahara, if I were a betting man, I've venture to say that you've probably been around the block a lot more than Dahlia has. And since she's going to be my wife, I think my name linked romantically to hers won't be a problem."

Zahara's eyes enlarged. "You're going to marry her?"

The man smiled. "They're waiting for you in wardrobe, Zahara. We've got a big scene to do. You should go get ready."

Zahara pressed herself against him a second time. "Yes, we do have a scene together," she said. "And isn't this the scene where we make love to each other?"

Guy shook his head. "No, this is the scene where we break up."

Gripping him by the front of his shirt she leaned in to kiss his mouth, eagerly gliding her lips over his lips. From the outside looking in, someone would have thought the two were sharing an intimate moment until Guy gripped her by the shoulders and pushed her from him. He shook his head vehemently.

"It's not going to happen, Zahara. Sorry!"

Zahara bristled. "It could be good between us."

He shrugged his broad shoulders. "I don't think so."

The woman stood staring at him for a brief moment before doing an about-face and stomping off. As a door slammed loudly behind her, Dahlia moved to Guy's side. After swiping at his mouth with the back of his hand, he wrapped his arms around her torso and hugged her tightly, planting a blatant kiss on her lips.

"What was that about?" Dahlia asked, her gaze shifting toward Zahara's exit.

Guy shook his head. "Nothing important. Just Zahara being Zahara."

Dahlia nodded slowly. "And was Guy being Guy?"

"Aren't I always?"

"For a second there it looked like you two were having a moment together."

"Looks can be deceiving."

"So you weren't making nice with that woman?"

"Nope!"

"And you were kissing her because…?"

"She kissed me. I had nothing to do with it. That's why she stormed off angry."

Dahlia shook her head. "Well, I guess it's a good thing that your last scene together is a fight."

Guy laughed. "I was just thinking the very same thing 'cause I have no doubt that she is going to be a beast!"

Dahlia had forgotten how much she enjoyed the energy of Venice Beach. And after the day she'd had with Zahara and her tantrums, the free-spirited atmosphere was just what she needed to help her unwind. As she walked the beachfront district on the west side of Los Angeles, she was grateful that all of the scenes Zahara shared with Guy were done, finished and in the can. It had been a long fourteen weeks and had she needed any more time to capture the two of them together she knew that it would have been next to impossible to accomplish.

Guy's blatant rejection had set Zahara right on edge; the woman did not take kindly to being ignored. For most of the day she'd been miserable with the rest of the cast and the crew, and it was only Dahlia's threat to pursue legal action against her that kept her from walking off set before the last scenes were done. But like Guy had predicted, Zahara's anger toward him played out wonderfully on film. And the moment Dahlia had shouted "cut" Zahara had disappeared without so much as a goodbye.

Dahlia sighed. She just knew that it was going to require a call from her attorney to Zahara's people to ensure Zahara showed up the following week to wrap up some voice-over work that Dahlia needed from her. The actress had made it perfectly clear that she was not going to make anything Dahlia needed from her easy.

Dahlia paused along the two-and-a-half-mile pedestrian-only promenade to watch one of the performers, a man dubbed King Solomon the Snake Charmer. The black man was bare-chested, dressed only in a native breechcloth and African kufi. He performed an acrobatic dance of sorts with a number of large snakes, and Dahlia was entertained by the children who were watching him in complete awe.

She then continued her stroll toward the basketball courts and the street ballers who were lost in competition. Guy saw her before she saw him, and his game face shifted into a wide grin. Letting his guard down for that brief moment enabled one of the other players to snatch the basketball from his hands and sail to the other end of the court to nail a basket. Guy's team shook their heads in dismay as they heckled him off the court.

"Put a sock in it," Guy shouted as he skipped to her side. Unable to mask his excitement, he swept her up into his arms and spun her around.

Dahlia laughed, wrapping her arms tightly around his neck. "Hey, you!"

"What took you so long, woman? I was just about to call out the troops to come look for you."

"It wasn't nice of you to break up with Zahara on the same day she announces that you two are an item. She was absolutely impossible to deal with after you left."

"That's what happens when you're dealing with crazy. I don't want any part of that woman's craziness, thank you."

Dahlia shook her head, still laughing. She pressed her lips to his and kissed him warmly. "I missed you," she said, her voice dropping an octave.

Guy grinned widely. "I missed you, too. Are you ready to eat? We can grab something now if you want."

She shook her head. "Not really. You can keep playing if you want. I don't mind waiting."

"I'm done," he said, moving to the bleachers to grab his belongings, a white hand towel and small gym bag. "They're making me look bad!" he shouted loudly as he waved a hand toward his friends.

One of the men pointed in his direction. "Yo, dude, you play like a girl!"

"I bet a girl plays better than you," another chimed in.

Flipping his hand in their direction, Guy shouted goodbye and grabbed Dahlia's hand, entwining his fingers between hers.

Resuming the walk down the promenade, Dahlia completely lost herself in the moment. The weather was picture-perfect with the cool breeze blowing inland off the water and the sun just beginning to drop low in the bright blue sky. She and Guy were chatting easily about everything and about nothing, and for the first time, Dahlia couldn't imagine herself needing or wanting anything more to sustain her.

She was just about to say so when a young man with a large camera stepped out in front of them, the flash going off with each image he snapped. Dahlia was only taken by surprise for a brief moment, too used to being accosted by the paparazzi when she least expected it. She felt Guy tighten his grip on her hand.

"Guy, Dahlia, can I get a picture?" the man asked, seeking permission well after the fact.

Guy shook his head. "You want a picture?" he asked.

"Yeah!"

Dropping his bag, Guy slid his arm around Dahlia's waist and pulled her close against him. Dropping his mouth to hers, he kissed her passionately, drawing the breath from her. In response, Dahlia wrapped her arms around his neck and kissed him back. The young photographer snapped shot after shot, a wide smile blooming across his face. "Thanks! Thanks a lot," he said eagerly.

When Guy finally drew back, his own bright smile beaming down at her, Dahlia laughed, knowing that before the next morning's sunrise, confirmation of their relationship was going to be splashed across every major newspaper and magazine.

Right out of the gate Guy knew that the most popular question asked would be about his relationship with Zahara and then with Dahlia. Having the opportunity to set the record straight on national television couldn't have come at a more opportune time, so when the *Good Morning America* host asked him just that, he was prepared with an answer.

Guy laughed modestly, crossing one leg over the other. "Zahara and I are good friends and we've had an amazing time together shooting *Passionate*. The chemistry between us has made for a wonderful movie, and I couldn't have asked for a more talented costar."

"So there is no truth to you two being an item?"

"It's all rumor." Guy laughed. "The script calls for you to kiss a woman on camera and suddenly the tabloids have you engaged and married."

The host laughed, too.

"And what about your film's director, is that rumor, as well?"

Guy smiled, taking notice of the camera that zoomed in for a close-up. "I don't know, George. What are they saying?"

"Well, to hear it told, you and Dahlia Morrow have also become exceptionally close."

Guy nodded. "Dahlia Morrow has been an exciting director to work for. I am very excited with the performance she was able to pull out of me. *Passionate* is going to be an incredible film."

"So are you saying that there is nothing going on between you two?"

"I'm saying that she is an amazing woman."

"So are you confirming that there is something going on between you two?"

Guy chuckled softly. "Let's just say, I didn't need a script to kiss Dahlia Morrow."

The rest of the entertainment interview focused on Guy's role in *Passionate,* his new men's line and whether or not he intended to reprise his James Bond role. When the host shook his hand and wished him well, Dahlia turned off her television set. Across town, Zahara did the same thing.

Moving to look out her window, Dahlia took a sip of orange juice and smiled. She loved everything about that man and he loved her. And without making a spectacle of them both, he'd let everyone else know.

From her own window, Zahara twisted her lips in a wide snarl. She didn't take kindly to Guy Boudreaux shutting her down for the likes of a woman like Dahlia. And she didn't take too kindly to him doing it so publicly. Taking a deep puff of her cigarette, Zahara blew rings of gray smoke into the air. No, she thought, she wouldn't take kindly to this at all.

Chapter 16

Standing buck naked in Dahlia's kitchen, Guy reached for a bottle of bourbon from an upper cabinet. Filling a heavy-bottomed, crystal glass, he tossed one shot back, then refilled it a second time.

Outside the sun had settled down for the night, and a blanket of dark filled the night sky. Stepping out onto the back patio, Guy stood beneath the shimmer of moonlight and took a deep breath of fresh air. A warm breeze washed over his naked body.

He slowly sipped his drink, thinking of Dahlia and the time they'd been sharing together. Since their first time, they'd spent more time in bed than out of it. Dahlia's newly discovered sexuality had opened a door of exploration and study that had taken them both on an intense sensual journey. Guy couldn't remember being with any woman who was as open to the avenues of sexual adventure that he and Dahlia had explored together. The woman had taken him to heights he hadn't even known to be possible. He grinned widely at the memories.

Together they'd discovered that Dahlia was a bit of an exhibitionist, and her spirited personality didn't stop her from pushing the boundaries. He'd been shocked when she'd straddled him in the front seat of his car while they'd sat parked in the darkened studio parking lot. With nothing but the faint glow of one lamppost shining in the distance and the risk of being caught by one of the studio security guards, she'd stroked him to a rock-hard erection, then had slid the line of her silk panties to the side and ridden him to orgasm. Both had been breathing heavily, fighting for composure, as the security guard had knocked at the driver's-side window, concerned that something might have been wrong.

He'd also not been prepared when he'd awakened to Dahlia having tied his hands to the bedposts, teasing him unmercifully. She had blown warm breaths against his erection, stretching it to new proportions. She'd been giddy with laughter as she'd tasted him for the first time, wrapping her lips and tongue around his manhood, suckling him to climax. Guy felt himself harden at the memory. He took a deep inhale of air and held it before releasing it slowly past his full lips. He took another sip of his drink.

There was no denying that Dahlia liked to have control, inside the bedroom and out of it. But tonight was going to be different. Tonight, Guy thought, Dahlia was going to have to relinquish control to him. She was going to have to trust him completely. When he'd said so he'd seen the hesitation in her eyes. Despite her reluctance, though, she'd nodded her consent, biting down nervously against her bottom lip, vulnerability seeping from her gaze. As the image flashed through his thoughts Guy was suddenly overcome with heat, lust washing over him with a vengeance.

He wrapped his left hand around the length of hardened steel between his legs as he downed the last drop of his drink. He chuckled softly, noting that he was probably more nervous than she was. Taking another deep breath, he stepped back inside and secured the door behind him. Shutting off the lights, he headed up to the master bedroom and Dahlia.

As he stepped into the room Guy couldn't help but think that she was a work of art, lying on her side, her knees pulled up to expose her throbbing privates. Her arms were bound behind her back, her eyes blindfolded, a gag secured in her mouth. Outside, that full moon peeked from beneath a sky of dark clouds, casting a low light through the room. The soft glow accentuated the soft creaminess of her delicate skin.

Dahlia jumped ever so slightly as she felt him approach the bed. She'd been lying in anticipation for at least twenty minutes, but it had felt like forever. She struggled slightly against the ties that confined her, her breathing becoming heavy. It was all too unnerving, and Dahlia was suddenly apprehensive. But it was Guy, and she trusted Guy. She took a deep breath and tried to relax.

Guy drew a slow finger down the length of her spine, his fingernail grazing her flesh. Dahlia gasped at the touch, her body quivering. Sliding his finger along the crack of her behind he felt her tremor with nervous anticipation, her excitement rising. He'd been teasing and taunting her since she'd clasped her hands behind her back and allowed him to secure them. But he hadn't truly touched her, not allowing her naked skin to have any contact with his.

"I love your breasts," he said as he drew the backs of his hands across the fleshy tissue. "They belong to me now, understand?" he said, his tone firm and commanding.

Dahlia nodded.

There was suddenly nothing from him, no movement, no sound, no touch, nothing. Dahlia shifted her head from side to side, thinking he'd left her alone again, and then suddenly he pushed her backward, the gesture rough as he leaned down and took her right breast into his mouth, his tongue eagerly making friends with her nipple. He began to lick and suck on it, making it hard. He repeated the action on her left nipple. As he sucked on one he would pinch and twist the other.

When he bit down on one of her nipples, Dahlia's body bucked, a hint of pain melding with a mountain of pleasure. If it were not for the gag in her mouth she would have screamed; instead, she grunted her desire loudly. Guy did it again to the other nipple, playing with them for some time, and Dahlia's desire was so intense she imagined that it would take little to nothing to bring her to orgasm. She clamped her knees tightly together.

After indulging himself for a few minutes Guy crawled off of her. The loss of his touch caused her to squirm with need. Guy stared down at her, stroking himself gently. He stepped back from the bed and paused, intent on making her ache with wanting. She panted heavily, grinding her pelvis in the air.

Guy grinned mischievously. Moving back to her side, his finger tapped at the crevice between her legs, where her sex was throbbing. She shuddered, her arousal rising with an intensity that was almost unbearable. He gently rotated the tip of his index finger over her erect clitoris, pulling and pushing it in slow but sure circles.

It felt so good that Dahlia found herself panting and sighing in pleasure as she quickly approached orgasm. She was trembling uncontrollably. Guy continued his ministrations, the slow and methodic teasing meant to prolong the inevitable for as long as he could. He stood above her as she rolled onto her side, allowing her legs to fall open. She pushed her hips forward, pumping his fingers into the moist, hot cavity and then she came, that final burst of pleasure making her collapse back into a fetal position, his hand clasped tightly between her thighs as she quivered unabashedly.

Guy allowed her to rest just long enough to catch her breath. When she was no longer panting heavily he rubbed her again, his fingers painting her secretions across her private space. He stuck a finger into the drenched tunnel and began to work it in and out. He could feel her arousal rising a second time, and when she began to press herself against his palm he slapped her between her legs, making her jump. He felt her gasp at the infraction, and he chuckled softly to himself. Then without comment he leaned down and started to lick her, flicking his tongue over her clit until her whole body began to tremble.

He sucked and nibbled at her until her body went stiff and then with a muffled moan Dahlia came hard a second time, her juices flowing abundantly as Guy continued to lap at her intimately. And then he stopped.

Guy didn't move, feeling her sexual tension evaporate, her breathing becoming slow and steady. When she had ceased shaking and relaxed, her anxiety suppressed, he reached to untie her gag. His fingers gently grazed her lips, and then slid across the length of her jawline. Dahlia leaned her cheek into the palm of his hand, and when she did he pulled his hand away.

"Guy…"

He pressed his index finger to her lips. "Shh…if you talk I'll gag you again," he said firmly.

Dahlia closed her mouth, pressing her lips tightly together.

"Good girl," Guy said as he leaned to give her a quick kiss. He trailed his hand down the side of her face. "Open your mouth," he commanded, fighting to sugarcoat his lust with gentleness.

Dahlia obliged, her lips parting slightly. Guy brushed the head of his sex over her lips, making her open her mouth even more as he tapped himself against her tongue. His excitement was palpable, the sexual tension so thick that you could have cut it with a knife.

He gripped the back of her head, his hands twisting through her hair. As he pumped his hips slowly in and out of her mouth, Dahlia licked and sucked him eagerly. It was pleasure beyond belief, more than he could have ever believed. When it became too much for him to bear, Guy pulled back, gulping air to stall the sensations sweeping through his body. When he'd regained his composure he carefully flipped her onto her stomach, pulling her up onto her knees. He pushed her head forward, pressing her face and breasts against the bed as he lifted her hips and bottom to his chest. He kissed one butt cheek and then the other before leaving a love bite against the firm flesh. When Dahlia yelped and wiggled anxiously, Guy slapped his palm against the lush tissue. Her body jumped, and she groaned into the mattress, her flesh stinging sweetly.

Guy smacked the other side, still pressing a heavy palm against the back of her head. And then he spanked her, slapping one cheek and then the other.

Tears misted Dahlia's eyes as she wiggled anxiously. Guy leaned in and kissed both cheeks, murmuring against her sore bottom.

"You are such a good girl, Dahlia," he whispered softly. "You promised me anything, remember? You said you'd do whatever I asked. Right, Dahlia?" he questioned as he untied the blindfold.

Dahlia moaned, focused only on Guy's hands as they lightly stroked the divide of her backside, fingers tapping and teasing places nothing had ever touched before.

"That's my good girl," Guy murmured excitedly as

he continued to stroke her from back to front and back again.

On the verge of yet another climax, Dahlia was whimpering and all but begging for his ministrations. Reaching for the condom he'd rested against the nightstand, Guy sheathed himself quickly. Crawling onto the bed behind her, he pressed his engorged member across her exposed flesh, rubbing the tip of his bulging erection against her until the head of his manhood was wet with her juices.

Taunting her, he tapped himself against her back entrance. Dahlia snapped her head to peer over her shoulder up at him. The safe word they'd agreed upon earlier was on the tip of her tongue, her eyes wide with anxiousness. As she met his stare Guy pointed his index finger at her and shook his head.

"Trust me," he mouthed as he continued to caress her easily.

Dahlia inhaled swiftly, her eyes bulging at the prospect of what he was proposing. Her body quivered with anticipation as Guy leaned to press a kiss against the curve of her back. Then, unable to resist a moment longer, he buried the length of himself deep in her sweet spot, her vaginal muscles locking like a vice around his hardness.

Dahlia moaned loudly as Guy slowly pulled himself back. He gripped her hips as he rammed himself forward then pulled back slowly a second time. With each thrust Dahlia throbbed uncontrollably and before long he was thrusting in and out of her with wild abandon. He was breathing hard and sweating profusely, skin slapping skin, and though he wanted to slow himself down, to tease her even more, she felt too good.

Dahlia screamed as Guy rode her hard and fast. "Deeper!"

It was only a matter of time before ripples of pleasure were pulsing through both of them and then they exploded, hitting an earthshaking orgasm simultaneously.

Guy collapsed on top of her and just lay there, unable to move for several minutes. Eventually he regained the strength to move, lifting himself up enough to untie Dahlia's hands. Wrapping his arms around her torso he massaged her limbs, restarting her circulation as he dropped back against her and pulled her tightly to him. The woman was still purring softly, still lost in the throes of the sensual pleasure she'd just experienced.

Guy kissed her cheek gently, and then he pressed his mouth to her ear.

His seductive tone was low and soft. "Next time," he promised as he tapped her backside gently. "I'm going there."

Dahlia's eyes flew open, her gaze moving to the oversize mirror across the way and the reflection of them lying comfortably together. She clenched and tightened, Guy's whispered words like starter fluid on a raging fire. The sweet ache between her legs returned and a wide smile blossomed across her face. As she contemplated the possibilities, both of them drifted off into a deep sleep.

Chapter 17

"You're a freak!" Leslie cried teasingly. Tears rolled down the woman's face as she laughed helplessly.

Her face hot with embarrassment, Dahlia laughed with her. She tossed a quick glance over her shoulder before responding, "I am not! Why do I have to be a freak for just asking if you've ever done that before?" Her voice was low and hushed as she whispered in her friend's direction.

"Because if you're asking about it, you're thinking about it. You go, girl! Get your freak on!"

Dahlia giggled, her grin wide and full. "I'm asking because I think women need to take command of their sexuality. Why shouldn't we be more adventurous in the bedroom?"

"That's just a little too adventurous for my blood. I tried it once with Marco, you remember him, right?"

Dahlia nodded.

"The problem I had was that Marco liked it just a bit too much. After a while it was the only thing he was ever interested in doing. He had to go."

Dahlia laughed. "What's the freakiest thing you've ever done with a man?"

Leslie shook her head. "I don't do things like that. I'm just a nice, sweet, missionary position kind of girl."

"I know that's a lie," Dahlia said. "You forget the time you forced me to go to that sex toy shop with you, don't you? 'Cause I remember the toys you went home with!"

Leslie pretended to slap her forehead. "It's my lie and I'm sticking to it," she said, falling into a fit of giggles for the umpteenth time.

Dahlia tossed another quick look over her shoulder, noting that a few members of the crew were stealing glances at them. Everyone seemed amused by the good time the two women were enjoying. She dropped her whisper two octaves. "I met Guy's family this weekend. We flew to New Orleans on his brother's private jet."

Leslie clapped her hands excitedly. "The parents! Now that means it's serious."

"It is serious," Dahlia said, shifting into the memories of her weekend excursion.

From start to finish the three-day trip had been its own adventure. Their antics had started shortly after takeoff, when the stewardess had handed Guy a soft blanket the color of corn silk. After they were high up in the midday sky, he'd settled down against her, his head resting on her shoulder, that blanket tossed over the two of them. Between conversations with the flight attendant and the copilot, Guy had slipped his hand beneath the hem of her skirt, his index finger teasing the lines of her lace thong.

His teasing had been slow and methodical as he'd ripped her panties from her hips, stuffing them into his pocket. And then he'd fingered her to orgasm as she'd fought to maintain her composure beneath the watchful eye of the flight crew. Before Dahlia could catch her breath Guy had pulled her to the lavatory and had pushed her against the wall, easing himself behind her. He'd pushed her skirt up and her blouse away and had taken her roughly, officially inducting her into the Mile High Club as he'd stroked her with long, hard strokes, her chest and face pressed tight to the tiled wall.

Dahlia inhaled swiftly at the memory, an intense wave of heat washing over her. She stole a quick glance toward Leslie, who was still chatting on about something Dahlia didn't have a clue about. A sly smile spread across her face.

Guy's family had welcomed her warmly, his mother, Katherine, and father, Mason "Senior" Boudreaux, were absolutely delightful. And then there had been the brothers she'd met at Spago, Kendrick, Donovan, Darryl and the oldest brother, Mason, and his wife, her good friend Phaedra. Plus his sisters, Tarah, Maitlyn and Kamaya, all questioning and assessing whether or not she was a good fit for the youngest boy in their large family. The only sibling she had yet to meet was his sister Katrina, the district court judge with the new baby married to the Stallion brother whose family had invested a handsome amount of money into her film.

When they'd found a moment to sneak away from the family, her sorority sister had pulled her aside, eyes wide with questions.

"So how long have you and Guy been an item?" Phaedra had asked in a hushed whisper as the two had stood on the Boudreaux family porch.

Dahlia had shrugged her shoulders, grinning broadly. "It happened fast. But he's been the best thing for me. I can't remember the last time I was this happy!" Dahlia had exclaimed.

Phaedra had giggled with her. "Have you two—" she paused "—you know?" she'd questioned.

Dahlia had laughed. "What?"

"You know," Phaedra had repeated, her eyebrows lifted teasingly. "Has Guy gotten into your cookie jar yet?"

Her friend had laughed again. "I don't believe you!"

Phaedra had laughed with her. "Just answer the question!"

Dahlia had shrugged, a deep blush painting her expression. But she hadn't responded.

Phaedra had clapped her hands together excitedly. "It's about time. 'Dem cookies was probably close to stale as long as you've been holding out."

"You sound like Leslie."

"Leslie and I are your sorority sisters. We know you!"

"Yes, you two are, so you know that Guy had to be very special for me to cross that line."

Phaedra had blown out a deep breath. "I know what you mean. I felt the same way about Mason."

"He's such a great guy, Phaedra. You two are perfect for each other."

Phaedra had grinned. "Yes, we are!" She'd suddenly jumped up and down excitedly. "We might be sisters-in-law," she'd exclaimed.

Guy had suddenly appeared from around the corner. "What are you two ladies up to out here?" he'd asked as he'd moved behind Dahlia and wrapped her in his arms.

Phaedra had still been grinning. "I was just telling Dahlia that if you two ever got married we would officially be family."

Guy had chuckled warmly. "You mean *when* Dahlia and I get married 'cause we are definitely getting married."

"And having babies to hear him tell it," Dahlia had teased.

"A baby. You know how *we* star couples do it," Guy had corrected.

Dahlia had shaken her head. "I swear, Guy, you don't have any sense!" She'd laughed.

Phaedra and Guy had laughed with her.

"Well, I know this, Mr. and Mrs. Star Couple," Phaedra had said. "I've got dibs on the first photos, wedding *and* baby."

"Of course," Guy had said. "We will definitely keep it in the family."

Phaedra had leaned over to give her friend and her brother-in-law a big hug. "I am so happy for you," she'd whispered against Dahlia's ear before she'd headed off to see what her husband and the rest of the family was up to in the backyard.

Guy had pulled Dahlia back into his arms, nuzzling his face into her neck. "So, I was missing you," he'd whispered softly.

Dahlia cuddled close to him. "Mmm," she'd purred as he'd kissed her mouth, his full lips cushioned against hers.

"You're trying to start something," she'd giggled softly.

"Yes, I am." Guy had shifted his body against hers, and Dahlia had felt the rise of his erection pressing hard against her body.

Dahlia had taken a quick glance around her, concerned that someone might be watching them. "You need to stop," she'd muttered nervously.

Guy had shaken his head. "You need to help me with my personal problem," he'd muttered back, still kissing her.

"I am not doing anything in your mother's house!"

Guy had laughed. "Yes, you are. Come on," he'd said, pulling Dahlia by the hand.

She'd moved inside the home behind him. In the distance she could hear the family laughing out in the rear yard. Guy had peaked out the kitchen window, then pulled her into the pantry and closed the door.

"You have lost your mind," Dahlia had exclaimed as he'd undone his pants and dropped them to the floor at his ankles. He'd pulled his T-shirt up and over his head, dropping it against one of the pantry shelves.

His head had waved from side to side, his face bright

with glee. He'd clasped a hand around his rising erection and shaken his manhood in her direction. "It needs help, Dahlia," he'd said, pouting like a two-year-old. "Please?"

Dahlia had suddenly been able to hear voices in the outer room. Her eyes had widened, and she'd been mortified at the prospect of them being caught by either of his parents or siblings. She'd gestured for him to put his clothes back on, and he'd ignored her, still waving his member for her attention.

He'd begun to stroke himself gently, his head falling back against his shoulders. He'd licked his lips, his hips beginning to pump slowly back and forth. The voices on the other side of the door had moved back outside, fading off into the distance.

Guy had opened his eyes and stared at her, the sexy look making her moist between her thighs. He had crooked his index finger in her direction and gestured for her to come to him. Like a snake being charmed, Dahlia had moved against him. Guy had clasped her face between his hands and then kissed her forehead, her nose and then her mouth.

"Guy," Dahlia had breathed, unable to resist.

Guy had drawn his hands through her hair, his fingers twisting in the strands. His lips had nuzzled her lips as he'd slipped his tongue between them. Dahlia had been breathing heavily, fighting not to squeal out loud. His erection had seemed to grow larger as it pressed tight to her abdomen. When Dahlia had returned the gesture, Guy had sucked her tongue into his own mouth, biting it gently with his teeth.

She'd been suddenly hungry for him, suckling the soft skin on his neck, kissing down to his broad shoulders, his rich chocolate tone like a decadent dessert against her tongue. Sliding her hands across his chest, she'd licked one nipple and then the other.

Guy had been panting and moaning as he'd dropped his palms against her shoulders and pushed her downward. As he had guided her to her knees, Dahlia had lifted her gaze to his. He'd nodded his desire, his sex waving eagerly for her attention. Her lips had tugged at the spray of dark pubic hair and then without a second thought she'd sucked him between her lips, her tongue lavishing him warmly. Guy had thrust his hips forward and began to rhythmically pound himself into her mouth.

Dahlia had clutched his hips as she'd guided him in and out past her lips. Guy had begun to pick up speed and then he'd suddenly cried out, clenched his buttocks and rammed forward, grinding his groin into her face. Guy had held his position, shuddering, bucking once, then twice, still clenching his backside as Dahlia lingered over his organ until he was drained dry and had begun to wilt. Then he'd pulled away, his body still shuddering with aftershock.

As Dahlia had come to her feet, she'd pulled his pants upward, their hands bumping as he zipped himself up and she tried to help. Dahlia had dabbed at her mouth with the hem of Guy's shirt before passing it back to him, her gaze still locked with his.

On the other side of the door they had been able to hear voices a second time, and Guy's eyes had widened, a wide grin spreading across his face. Dahlia shook her head a second time. When the voices had once again disappeared, she'd leaned her body close to his, dropping into the warmth of his embrace. Guy had pressed his lips to her ear and whispered, his voice low and deep.

"Your turn," he'd said, and before she had realized what was happening Guy had slipped warm, insistent fingers inside the waistband of her pants and down into her panties.

Dahlia had moaned softly as she'd parted her legs, instinctively offering herself to him. He'd diddled her easily, and then he'd thrust three fingers deep into her moist canal. As she'd squeezed his fingers in a convulsion of lust and he'd swirled them deep inside the slick, sticky walls, Dahlia had fathomed that she might pass out from the pleasure. It had only been Guy's arm locked tight around her waist, holding her close to him, that kept her standing. With lewd abandon Guy had fingered her until she'd crashed and burned in an inferno of orgasmic bliss.

As she'd fought to catch her breath, Guy had kissed her deeply, then the two had let out a fit of giggles. Noise right outside the door had suddenly been too close for comfort.

"Fix your clothes," Guy had whispered, trying to help her button her slacks and straighten the cotton blouse she'd worn.

Glowing with sexual sweat, the duo had fought to put their clothes back in place and then the pantry door had suddenly swung open.

Eyes wide, Guy and Dahlia had both turned to stare, their guilty gazes meeting his sister Tarah's curious stare. Tarah had suddenly closed the door, her mother's voice ringing loudly behind her.

"What are you doing, Tarah? Get the canned corn," Mrs. Boudreaux had said as she pulled a bowl from one of her cabinets.

Opening the pantry door Tarah had shaken her head slowly, unable to hide the amusement across her face. She'd held out her hand and Guy had passed her two cans of corn from the shelf. As she'd taken them from him she'd shaken her finger at them both, still grinning widely.

Over her shoulder she'd called for her mother's attention. "Mom, Dad just called for you."

"No, he didn't," they'd heard the older woman answer. "Did he?"

"I heard him," Tarah had insisted as she'd moved to the woman's side, resting the cans on the counter. "He called you."

Katherine Boudreaux had sighed with exasperation. "I swear," she'd said as she'd moved out of the kitchen and back outside.

As they'd heard the screen door slam behind her exit, Guy had pulled Dahlia out of the enclosure.

"Thanks, Tarah!" he'd mouthed, waving at his sister.

"You know y'all are wrong, Guy!" she'd cried. "Y'all are too wrong!"

With the memory swirling through her mind, Dahlia suddenly laughed out loud.

Leslie eyed her suspiciously. "It really wasn't that funny," she said.

"I'm sorry," Dahlia apologized. "I was just thinking about something Guy did on our trip."

Leslie shook her head knowingly. "Yep! It is definitely serious with you two."

Chapter 18

For three days Zahara and Dahlia went back and forth on the sound bites that Dahlia needed her to complete. As always, Zahara was a force to be reckoned with, determined to do what she wanted, only when she wanted.

Dahlia let out a deep sigh as she reclined back against her chair. Dave, the sound engineer seated beside her, was becoming equally frustrated as Zahara carried on a cell phone conversation with someone about absolutely nothing important. He turned up the microphone as they continued to listen in.

"And I told him I wasn't about his small-town life," Zahara was professing. "I don't roll like that. If he couldn't keep me at the lifestyle to which I've become accustomed, then there was no way in hell he was going to be wasting my good time. I mean, for real!"

Dahlia leaned forward and pressed the intercom button into the sound booth. "Zahara, we need—"

Zahara cut her off. "I said I needed a quick minute, Dahlia. This is important," she responded curtly.

The soundman chuckled. "Yeah," he muttered under his breath. "We all know what she had for breakfast is so important."

Dahlia cut an eye in his direction. "She is unbelievably ridiculous," she muttered back. She leaned forward and depressed the intercom button a second time. "Zahara, if you do not get off the phone so we can finish this I will begin to deduct the studio time from your wages. It's your choice." She leaned back in her seat, crossing her arms over her chest.

"Aw, sookie, sookie now," Dave teased. "She's about to blow!"

"Yes, I am," she said.

From inside the sound booth Zahara glared openly. She said goodbye to the party on the other end of her phone line. Tossing her cell phone into her leather bag, she stood with her hand on her hip. "What?" she mouthed, meeting the look Dahlia was giving her.

Dahlia pressed the intercom one last time. "Thank you. Take it from the top," she said, gesturing for Dave to fill in the back sounds as they began to record.

Like the professional she could have been Zahara delivered her lines easily. For the next hour she stayed in character and on point. Dahlia marveled at how she so easily became her character, likable and lovable, her story moving an audience to tears. Then, just like that,

Zahara was herself, mean-spirited, self-centered and a royal pain in everyone's nether regions.

"Now what?" Zahara exclaimed, a hand frozen against the line of her lean hips.

"We're going to take a quick break and then I just need to get a few more audio lines from you and we'll be done," Dahlia responded.

Reaching for her phone, Zahara turned her back to them, dialed and resumed her conversation.

Dave shook his head. "I need the toilet," he said, rising from his seat.

Dahlia nodded. "Take ten," she said.

At that moment Guy poked his head into the studio, then eased the rest of his body inside. He slapped palms with the man who was headed out the door, the two greeting each other warmly.

"Hey, beautiful," he cooed as he pressed a kiss against her cheek.

Dahlia reached up to wrap her arms around the man's neck. She kissed his lips. "You are a sight for sore eyes," she said sweetly.

Guy dropped down into the seat that Dave had vacated. "What's wrong? You look like you've had a hard day."

She rolled her eyes toward the sound room, gesturing in Zahara's direction. She didn't need to explain.

Guy shook his head. "Sorry that's a problem for you, baby," he said. He slid his seat closer to hers and hugged her tightly.

Leaning into the embrace, Dahlia suddenly felt as if all was well with the world. She felt immensely loved and wanted and there was nothing that the likes of Zahara Ginolfi could do that would ruin her good mood. She blew a gentle sigh against Guy's neck.

"I'll be done here in an hour or so. You interested in dinner?"

Guy grinned, dropping a hand to her knee. "Only if I can start with dessert," he teased.

Dahlia laughed. "You are just too fresh!"

For the next ten minutes the couple teased and flirted with each other. Neither bothered to pay Zahara an ounce of attention, but Zahara was intensely focused on the two of them. If either had bothered to pay any attention they would have heard the woman in the sound room, her cell phone conversation anything but casual.

"He'll be yesterday's news as soon as we're done with this film," Zahara was saying. "Everyone knows her relationships don't last longer than a few minutes. Anything longer than seventy-two days and she'd be setting a record." Zahara laughed. "Cheap trick. I can't stand those two. If you want gossip about 'dem two I can give you gossip!"

Minutes later, Guy excused himself from the room and Dahlia and Dave went back to work. On cue, Zahara turned on her star quality, again delivering her lines nicely. When she was done she eyed Dahlia smugly.

"That was perfect," Dahlia said, smiling politely. "Nice job, Zahara. I appreciate the effort. That's a wrap."

Rising from her seat, Zahara stormed out of the sound booth, heading in the direction of the dressing rooms. Before she made her exit she called Dahlia's name, slapped the right cheek of her backside and flipped the woman the bird.

"Thank you!" Dahlia responded behind her, shaking her head with disgust. "Thank you very much, Zahara."

Dave laughed as he pushed and pulled at the sound board dials. "We've got some good stuff here," he said. "Do you want to get started on the edits tonight?"

Glancing down at her watch, Dahlia shook her head. "No. We'll work on it tomorrow. Go home to your wife."

Dave smiled. "Thanks. She'll appreciate that. You have a good night," he said as he picked up his belongings and headed in the direction of the door. Then he called her name.

"Yes, sir?"

Dave laughed as he kissed his palm and slapped his wide butt, imitating Zahara's exit. "You know I had to do it." He chuckled heartily.

Shaking her head, Dahlia flipped her hand at him, sending him out the door. She laughed with him, listening to the sound of his mirth echoing in the distance. After the day the two had had, she was glad that they could find something about it to laugh at.

"Just for the record, Dahlia, I think it's very unprofessional of you to be flaunting your personal relationship on set. And I have no qualms about saying so publically."

Dahlia turned to where Zahara stood blowing rings of smoke into the air. Her accusing tone grated on Dahlia's last good nerve. "Zahara, what is your problem?" she questioned, both hands falling to her hips. "Specifically, what is your problem with me?"

Zahara moved out of the shadow she'd been standing in, moving into the light where Dahlia could see her. "I don't like you," she said as she took another slow drag of her cigarette then flicked the ash on the floor.

"Well, the feeling is mutual, so it's a good thing that our professional relationship is now done. And I've told you before that there is no smoking in this building."

Zahara took one last drag before she dropped her cigarette butt to the floor, twisting it beneath the toe of her high-heeled shoe. She blew the smoke in Dahlia's direction, the wealth of it billowing in her face. "I made this movie," Zahara said finally. "You need to remember that. Without me, *Passionate* wouldn't be anything but dribble."

Dahlia bit her tongue, instinctively wanting to tell Zahara Ginolfi exactly what she thought of her. But she didn't, knowing that was exactly what Zahara wanted. Dahlia had no doubts that were she to go off on Zahara Ginolfi it would show up on the internet before she got the last word out. Instead, she did what she knew would irritate Zahara the most. She agreed with her.

"You're right, Zahara. Without you there would be no movie."

For a brief moment Zahara stood with her mouth open, her eyes blinking. "I know," she said finally.

"Well, now that we have that established, I don't think there's anything else we need to say to one another. You have a good life, Zahara."

Zahara sucked her teeth. "It won't last."

"What won't last?"

"You and Guy. He deserves better. I'm sure he'll figure that out soon."

Dahlia smiled. "He already has," she said as she pointed toward the studio exit. "And I'm sure he appreciates your concern. Now, if you don't mind, I need to finish up here so that I can leave. Have a good night."

Zahara watched as Dahlia turned her back and continued to pack her personal possessions. With one last look in her direction, Dahlia disappeared back into the sound booth.

Lighting another cigarette, Zahara savored the flavor of the first inhale, filling her lungs before blowing the stale air out past her thin lips. After the second drag she turned an about-face and headed for the exit, moving out into the evening air.

Guy Boudreaux sat in his car talking on his cell phone. With the top down he was reclined back in the front seat as soft jazz played on his car stereo system.

He met Zahara's stare, tossed her a quick nod of his head and resumed his conversation, clearly not interested in conversing with her. Feigning disinterest, Zahara tossed her cigarette to the ground and headed for her own car. She was done with him, too.

Guy stole a quick glance at the digital clock in the dashboard. It had been well over thirty minutes since Dahlia had sent him a text message to say that she would only be a few minutes more. After he saw Zahara leave he would have gone inside to wait for her, but a call from his brother Darryl had held him hostage for longer than he would have liked. He was suddenly aware of it taking longer for Dahlia to come out than it should have.

"Hey, Darryl, let me call you back," he said into his earpiece. "I need to go find Dahlia."

"No problem," Darryl responded. "Thanks for listening."

"Anytime. And really, you need to listen to Mason. Asia is not the right woman for you. You need to let her go and stop trying to fix what's broke."

"I hear you," Darryl acknowledged. "I'll call you after she and I talk."

Just as Guy disconnected the call, one of the studio's security vehicles rounded the corner, coming to a screeching halt in the parking space beside him. In the distance he could hear the distinct sound of sirens drawing closer. The uniformed officer jumped out, excitedly pointing in the direction of the studio door. Panic suddenly washed over Guy. As the man rushed to his side, Guy looked toward where he pointed, noticing the smoke that billowed from the building for the first time.

Dahlia coughed; the smoke seeping beneath the closed door was beginning to take its toll. Outside, flames had engulfed the space, the fire consuming everything in its path. Dahlia had smelled the smoke first and when she'd gone in search of its source her path out had been blocked by the rapid rise of an inferno. With her purse and cell phone on the other side of the blaze there had been no way for her to call for help, and all she could do was wish and pray that something had triggered an alarm outside.

The temperature was beginning to rise with a vengeance. Sweat poured down Dahlia's face, mixing with the tears that seeped from her dark eyes. All she could think of was Guy and all they'd planned for their future together. Everything he'd teased about was about to go up in flames, and she hadn't even had the opportunity to tell him how much the possibility had meant to her.

Cowering in the corner of the room, Dahlia clutched her knees to her chest and rocked her body back and forth. It wasn't supposed to end this way, she thought, wishing she'd had an opportunity to say goodbye, wishing she'd been able to tell him just how much she loved him.

As the smoke rose Dahlia's cough erupted into waves of nausea and vomiting. Her face burned, and she couldn't catch her breath. Confusion washed over her and all she wanted to do was sleep. Falling over onto her side, she curled her body into the fetal position, her tears drying as quickly as they fell from her eyes. As she felt herself beginning to drift off, she called out to Guy, wishing for him to come to her. In the distance she imagined that she heard him calling her name.

Guy could hear the voices, family and friends postulating about things being well, tones of sympathy meant to ease his anguish. He had the sense of his body being badly bruised, but the drugs that clouded his thoughts were keeping the pain at bay. And though he was acutely aware of the commotion happening around him all he could focus on was Dahlia.

But Dahlia wasn't there. And he couldn't reach her.

And yet, his name on her tongue rang like sweet nectar against his ears. He called her name again and again, hopeful that he would be heard, and she would be there back in his arms where she belonged.

But all he heard from the voices were admonishments that Dahlia was well, they would both be fine and he needed to do nothing but rest. But respite was the last thing on his mind because Guy knew that until Dahlia was back in his arms nothing was going to soothe his soul.

Chapter 19

Neither Maitlyn nor Leslie were interested in managing the media. Both were grateful for the Communications Department at Cedars-Sinai Hospital; their team of professionals fielded all questions about how Guy Boudreaux and Dahlia Morrow were doing. At the request of their family they were releasing no details, respecting their right to privacy during their difficult time.

Clutching a cup of coffee between the palms of her hands, Leslie fought back the urge to cry, her foot tapping anxiously against the floor. Maitlyn paced from one side of the hospital waiting room to the other, fighting a wealth of nerves. Every so often they'd lock gazes, neither believing that such a tragedy could have put them in this moment.

The quiet was suddenly interrupted by the entrance of the Boudreaux family, Guy's parents and siblings joining them as they waited for news. Maitlyn fell into her father's arms, her tears finally falling as she released the hurt that had weighed down her spirit. She cried, and the patriarch held her until she was able to give them information about her brother's condition.

Leslie was also grateful for their arrival as she clung to her friend Phaedra and Guy's brother Mason, the two sensing that she too needed to be hugged and held.

"How's my baby?" Katherine Boudreaux questioned, fighting back her own tears.

"Tell us what happened," Senior commanded, pulling his daughter down to sit in a cushioned seat beside him.

Maitlyn swallowed hard, swiping at her eyes with a tissue before she answered. "There was a fire at the studio. Apparently, when it started Guy was outside waiting to pick up Dahlia. Dahlia was trapped inside, and the fire department says that before anyone could stop him Guy rushed into the building to try to get to her."

Maitlyn took another deep breath before continuing. "They say the ceiling collapsed, and Guy became trapped beneath one of the beams. They were able to get them both out though…."

"Oh, my God!" Mrs. Boudreaux exclaimed, pulling a closed fist to her mouth. "I need to see him. Where's my baby?"

Maitlyn shook her head. "They won't let us see him yet, Mama. They both suffered severe smoke inhalation, and the doctors say Guy suffered some serious burns."

Mason moved to his mother's side, leaning to kiss her forehead as he squeezed her hands. He tapped a heavy hand against his father's back. "I'll go find out what's going on," he said, gesturing for Kendrick to join him.

Tarah moved to Leslie's side, extending her hand in introduction. "Does Dahlia have family that we can call?"

Leslie nodded. "I've left messages for her brothers. I'll keep trying to reach them."

Mrs. Boudreaux nodded. "As long as she's here, she'll have family with her. We're her family, too, and we're not going anywhere until they're both ready to leave this hospital."

Leslie struggled to smile, her head bobbing up and down against her shoulders. Phaedra rubbed her gently against her back. "It's going to be okay," she said to her friend. "Dahlia is going to be okay."

"They both are," Katrina Stallion intoned, introducing herself and her husband, Matthew.

Minutes later Mason and Kendrick returned, a doctor in tow. The family came to their feet as he gave them a quick update on the condition of both of their loved ones.

"Mr. and Mrs. Boudreaux, my name is Dr. Mawaan Sharma. I was the admitting physician for your son and his fiancée. Mr. Boudreaux has been transferred to our burn unit. Your son suffered smoke inhalation, as well as second- and third-degree burns over forty percent of his body, mainly to his torso, arms and hands. Right now we have him fully sedated to minimize his pain levels. Under the circumstances he's doing exceptionally well, but obviously his condition is serious and he has a long recovery ahead of him."

"Can we see him?" Mrs. Boudreaux asked.

The doctor shook his head. "Soon. Right now we need to be concerned about infection, so we need to minimize all contact with him."

"What about Dahlia?" Leslie questioned, her voice a loud whisper.

"Ms. Morrow is in ICU for the time being. She suffered severe smoke inhalation, as well. She and Mr. Boudreaux both are undergoing inhalation therapy. Ms. Morrow is fortunate that the few burns she suffered were minimal. We anticipate she'll make a full recovery and be as good as new in a few weeks. We'll keep you updated if anything changes," Dr. Sharma said as he made his way out of the room.

Senior wrapped his wife in a deep embrace. "Everything's going to be fine," he whispered into her ear. "Just fine."

His wife nodded. "All you kids need to be in prayer," she said softly. "We all need to be praying for your brother and for Dahlia. We all need to be praying."

As the family sat vigil in the waiting room, Kendrick flipped channels on the television, searching for something that might divert their attention if only for a brief moment.

"Kendrick, turn back," Maitlyn suddenly shouted, jumping from her seat.

Everyone turned toward the TV, and Kendrick flipped back to catch the evening's newscast. The station broadcasted an image of Guy and Dahlia in a quiet embrace. He turned up the volume so they could all hear.

"Ash from a cigarette sparked a huge fire at the former Trinity Film Studio in Hollywood, officials said at a press conference yesterday. A cigarette butt discarded in a pile of trash on the studio floor smoldered before igniting freshly painted stage sets in the late evening hours.

"According to investigators the fire grew to engulf the two-story facility, causing it to burn to the ground despite the efforts of firefighters, who battled it for over three hours.

"Award-winning movie producer Dahlia Morrow and actor Guy Boudreaux were rescued from the burning building, but suffered smoke inhalation and severe burns. The fire has shocked the film community where both dominated the movie industry. Recently linked romantically, the duo was filming Ms. Morrow's latest movie, *Passionate,* starring Mr. Boudreaux and award-winning vocalist Zahara Ginolfi. No one has been charged, police have said. The status of the couple's condition is unknown. We'll have more information on the story as it develops.

"In other news…"

For two weeks Dahlia lay in bed, impatient for news of Guy and his progress. Leslie and Phaedra carried updates when they came, but Dahlia was anxious to see him for herself, to see Guy and know that he was okay.

Leslie informed her that Guy's condition had finally been upgraded from critical to good and all of his family had been allowed to visit and see him at least once. Also, that his mother had maintained a vigil by his bedside, intent on not leaving the hospital until the day Guy was able to leave with her.

After three weeks Dr. Sharma finally cleared Dahlia to leave her room, granting her permission to see for herself that Guy, too, was getting better. Sitting in a wheelchair outside his room, peering through the open door, Dahlia knew that since they'd arrived his family had declared a positive energy campaign around both of their recoveries. No one was allowed to cry in his presence, or hers, and everyone permitted to see them was only allowed to give the two of them positive affirmations.

One nurse who'd deigned to suggest that it was a waste of time for the family to talk to him while he'd been in an induced coma was removed from Guy's care so quickly that it had probably made the woman's head spin. Guy's mother and sisters had insisted everyone continue to talk to him, to uplift him with their energy, whether he could hear them or not.

Since his arrival in the burn unit Guy had survived two surgeries to remove the burned skin from his torso and arms. He'd had just as many to graft new skin in its place. Dahlia knew that the next month or so would involve long hours of painful therapy to get him back to the point where he was as good as new. Dahlia couldn't fathom how Guy endured. But he did. And as she sat watching him, she saw that he was enduring it with much love and laughter.

As he caught sight of her in the entrance, Guy's eyes widened with joy. He'd been desperate to see her as much as she'd wanted to see him, and he'd been anxiously waiting for the day the doctors gave her permission to come to his side, since he was unable to go to hers.

"Hey, you!" he called excitedly, wincing slightly as a wave of pain shot through his body. He grinned broadly, waving for her to come inside.

"Hey, yourself," Dahlia responded as she rolled herself through the door, coming to a stop at his bedside. She reached out a hand to gently caress the fingers that were not covered by bandages. His brother Kendrick and sister Kamaya both greeted her warmly.

"We'll give you two a little privacy," Kamaya said, gesturing for her twin to follow.

Kendrick winked an eye as he closed the door behind them.

Dahlia stood to press her mouth to his, grateful to feel his lips on hers once again. "I missed you so much," she whispered, tears misting her eyes.

Guy met her gaze. "Not nearly as much as I missed you. Are you doing okay, Dahlia? I was really worried. I just wanted to reach you, baby, but the fire... I tried and I couldn't find you and..."

Dahlia pressed her index finger to his lips to stall the words. "I know you did, and when you get better I'm going to give you a good slap for putting yourself in danger like that. But for now, I'm fine. They're going to release me tomorrow. We need to be worried about you. How are you doing?"

Guy shrugged. "I've been better. But hey, just think, it's going to be one heck of a vacation!"

"Has Dr. Sharma said how much longer you'll have to be here?"

"At least another week, but I'm doing really well."

Dahlia took a deep breath. "I love you so much! I can't believe this happened to us."

"I can't believe that I can't touch you," he said, gesturing with his bandaged arms.

Dahlia smiled. "You have a lifetime to touch me, Guy Boudreaux."

"You sure you still want me, woman? I mean, with me being all crispy and everything?"

She rolled her eyes then looked directly into Guy's eyes. "Of course, I *still* want you. And I'm not going anywhere," she said, her eyes glistening as she stared deeply into his. "Like it or not, you're stuck with me forever, Guy Boudreaux."

Guy grinned back. "I really like the sound of that." He pursed his lips, gesturing for a kiss. When Dahlia kissed him again, he grinned broadly. "I really do!"

Day in and day out Dahlia was by Guy's side. Despite being released from doctors' care herself, Dahlia ate, slept and lived wherever Guy was. His hospital room became her home, her bed a single cot tucked away in the corner. Despite the admonishments of his nursing staff to let them aid and care for him, Dahlia refused to not be there in case he needed her. From feedings to baths, to ensuring his medication was dispensed on schedule, there was nothing that she wasn't willing to do for him.

When the doctors were ready for him to be moved from the hospital to a rehabilitation facility for a brief two-week stay, Dahlia sought out the best care facility in the state of California, ensuring that everything he needed was at his disposal.

"You are going to spoil me," Guy said as Dahlia helped him to lift his legs back onto the bed and covered him with a white sheet.

"Good. That's what I want to do."

Guy shrugged, the bend to his lips failing. Dahlia sensed that something was weighing heavily on his spirit.

"Guy, what's wrong? Are you feeling okay?"

He shrugged a second time. "I feel fine. I just…" He hesitated, his gaze skirting over her face.

"What's wrong, darling?"

"I feel like I've become a burden to you, and it bothers me," he said.

She quickly shook her head. "How could you ever think such a thing?"

"There's just so much you should be doing, so much life you should be living, and instead, you're here every day taking care of me."

"I love you. Where else would I be? I'm here because I want to be here, Guy Boudreaux. Why are you being so silly?"

"When's the last time you worked on your movie?" he queried.

She paused, taking a deep breath. "The movie will get finished when you're well and we can both go back to working on it."

He took a deep breath and sighed. "Dahlia, I know how much *Passionate* means to you. Your work is everything so don't—"

She cut off his thought. "You are everything to me, and if you don't know that yet then I need to work harder to show you. Now," Dahlia said definitively, "you need to get over yourself. This pity party is done and finished or I'm going to wail on your backside."

Guy shook his head, his smile lifting ever so slightly. "That sounds promising. Would you rub it afterward?"

Dahlia shook her head in exasperation. "You are just too much."

"I'm horny, and I've been missing you."

"That has actually been on your mind?"

"Every day. You keep shaking your stuff at me and then you leave me hanging."

She laughed. "It's not like we could do anything right now."

"Says who? My stuff didn't get burned. My stuff is doing just fine. Come see."

She giggled. "What do you mean come see?"

"Come see my stuff," he said gesturing beneath the covers. "I need help with this personal problem."

Moving closer to his side Dahlia crawled onto the bed with him, easing her hand beneath the covers; a rising erection greeted her fingers. She pulled her hand back, her eyes widening.

"I don't want to hurt you," she said.

"Then you better get to work!" Guy persisted. He dropped back against the pillows. "I'm in pain," he exclaimed as he drew the back of his hand to his forehead, his eyes closed. "I need some relief!" He opened one eye to peek at her, nodding down to the extension that tented his bedclothes.

There was suddenly a knock on the room's door. Guy cursed under his breath. "I'll be damned," he groaned as he grabbed a pillow and dropped it into his lap. "Tell whoever that is that I was just about to get me some," he whispered, his eyes wide with frustration.

Dahlia laughed. "What if it's your mother?"

"Then I'll tell her myself."

Dahlia flipped her hand at him. "Oh, no, you won't," she said as she moved to answer the persistent tapping. As she swung the door open she was surprised to find Zahara Ginolfi standing on the other side.

"Zahara?"

The woman stood sheepishly, a massive bouquet of flowers in hand. "Dahlia, I hope I'm not interrupting."

Dahlia tossed Guy a quick glance. The man stared curiously, jutting his shoulders skyward. She took a step aside and gestured for Zahara to enter.

Moving into the space, Zahara looked painfully nervous. She looked from one to the other, smiling politely. "Guy, how are you?" she asked as she noted the compression bandage that covered his torso.

Guy winced. "In pain," he exclaimed loudly.

Dahlia fought not to laugh out loud. "Your meds are coming, honey," she said nonchalantly.

Zahara dropped the floral arrangement on the table

at Guy's side. "Should I call someone?" she asked, concern ringing in her tone.

"No, thank you. Dahlia has it under control." Guy then looked in Dahlia's direction.

Dahlia nodded, turning her attention toward their guest. "So, what brings you here, Zahara?" she asked.

The woman took a deep breath, her hands twisting nervously in front of her. "I needed to come see for myself that both of you were doing well. And I wanted to apologize."

Guy cut an eye at Dahlia, then refocused his stare on Zahara. "Apologize? For what?"

A tear rained down Zahara's cheek. "I think I'm responsible for the fire. I swear, I didn't mean for it to happen. I just wasn't thinking when I dropped that cigarette butt. I was certain that I put it out but…" She paused, her one tear melting into a fountain that dampened the front of her silk blouse.

Dahlia moved back to Guy's side and took his hand. She lifted it to her lips and kissed his fingers. Guy nodded his head slowly.

Zahara continued. "My attorney and I are meeting with the police and fire department. If this is my fault I want to make things right. I'm really not a bad person," she proclaimed, swiping at her eyes with the back of her hand.

"Zahara, we appreciate you stopping by," Guy said calmly. "And I appreciate you taking responsibility for your actions. But no matter what or who caused the fire, Dahlia and I are just grateful that we are both doing well and that we are both here together to one day tell our children our story."

Zahara nodded. "I really am sorry," she repeated, contrition blanketing her expression. She headed back to the door when Dahlia called after her. "Yes?"

"When we're ready to start promoting *Passionate* I hope that you'll be on board. You really did do an amazing job."

Zahara smiled, nodding her head up and down. "Definitely. Whatever you need."

As she made her exit, Dahlia followed her to the door, watching as she eased her way down the hall. Everything about the other woman's demeanor suggested that maybe Zahara had meant what she'd said. Dahlia then closed the door and locked it behind her and moved back to Guy's side.

"What do you make of that?" he asked, eyeing her curiously.

Dahlia shrugged her shoulders. "I don't have time to think about it," she said as she reached back beneath the covers. "It's time for your medication."

Guy gasped as she took him in the palm of her hand and began to stroke him gently. His breathing was erratic as he shifted his legs apart and eased his pelvis forward. "Good golly," he exclaimed loudly. "This is the kind of medicine I like!"

The telephone ringing pulled Guy out of a deep sleep. With his eyes closed he reached for his cell phone with one hand, pulling it into his palm. With his other he tapped the empty bed beside him, suddenly aware that Dahlia was no longer there with him.

"Hello?"

"Good morning, Son-shine!" Katherine Boudreaux sang into the receiver. "Were you sleeping?"

"Hey, Mama! No, I was just getting up."

The older woman laughed. "No you weren't, boy. You were sleeping!"

Guy laughed. "Yes, ma'am! How are you?"

"I'm good, baby. Just checking on you and Dahlia. I was reading the newspaper and saw a review of your new movie. They're saying good things about you and Dahlia."

Guy smiled. "That's good to hear. Really good to hear."

"And Daddy and I watched the Oscar predictions this morning. They say you and Dahlia will probably both get nominations. Isn't that exciting! I can't wait to see the movie when it premieres!"

Guy smiled, sitting up in the bed for the first time. "Thank you, Mama. That means a lot to us both."

The matriarch smiled into the receiver. "You're doing okay? Nothing hurting you or anything?"

"I'm good. You would never know I'd been in an accident," he said. "So you need to stop worrying, Mom!"

"You're my baby. I am always going to worry."

Guy smiled. "Everyone else doing okay?"

"The family is good. Daddy's still mean. We were in Dallas last week with Katrina and Matthew. They bought Collin a new car for his birthday."

"Now, that's what I'm talking about. Tell my sister I could use a new car, too."

His mother laughed. "He drives real good. Took his old grandma shopping while I was there."

"And the baby?"

"Getting fat as a tick. He looks like you did as a baby. I couldn't get enough of him. We plan on going back in a few weeks. Maybe you and Dahlia could come meet us."

Guy nodded into the receiver. "We might just do that."

"Are you keeping an eye on Maitlyn? I'm worried about your sister."

"She's hanging in there, Mama. I know the divorce isn't easy on her but she's keeping herself busy which means she's keeping me busier. That's one hardworking woman."

"I keep praying that she will find a man to love her the way she deserves. You and Dahlia don't have any nice friends you can introduce her to?"

He laughed. "I"ll see what we can do about that," he said, knowing that Maitlyn would have an absolute fit if they tried to play matchmaker with her.

"You do that and keep Tarah and Kamaya in mind, as well. I'm past ready for some more grandbabies! Well, son, I need to run. I just wanted to check on you."

"What are you up to that you have to rush off?"

"Darryl and Mason are coming home this afternoon. Darryl is going to build Mason's new office here in N'Orleans. I'm making my gumbo for dinner."

"I want some gumbo!"

His mother chuckled warmly. "I'm sure Darryl will be flying back to California soon. I'll make sure he brings you some."

"You need to show Dahlia how to make it," he said. "Give her something to do. She doesn't feed me, Mama. I've got to do all my cooking myself."

Katherine chuckled warmly. "I really do like that girl!"

Chapter 20

Guy always forgot just how hot Dahlia liked her showers. It had been almost six months since everything in their lives had changed, and since he'd been released from the rehab center they'd been trying to regain some normalcy to their lives. Dahlia had gone back to editing and finishing her movie and once Guy's sponsors had been convinced that he was well and able, they'd put him back to work; two photo shoots, a commercial, a Nike endorsement and one more blockbuster sequel were already in the works.

He caught a glimpse of his reflection in the bathroom mirror. The last reminder of the fire was a slim band of leathery flesh that ran from the top of his shoulder down his back, with just a hint of scarring across his chest. He was back in the gym with his trainer, and his abs were hard and rippled again, rigid muscles hailing his taut physique.

As he stepped into the shower, he reached around the beautiful woman to adjust the flow of water that rained down above their heads. Dahlia's hot was just a tad too hot for his comfort. As he reached his arm around her, she leaned up to press her mouth to his. The full length of her body crushed his as she pushed him back against the tiled shower wall. Water rained down over their bodies. Guy's hands glided across her back, her hips, her stomach, then settled against her full breasts, kneading them unabashedly.

He slid his fingers up to her neck to cup her face, his tongue dancing between her lips. He felt her pelvis pumping rhythmically against his, inciting a long length of erection between his legs. Dahlia's hands rested beneath his arms, pressed against the wall behind them, her body pressed tight to his.

Guy ran one hand back down between their stomachs and into the warm crevice between her thighs. Her wetness had nothing to do with the moisture from the water; Dahlia's core was searing hot and slick against his fingers. He rolled two fingers over her clit, marveling as it swelled beneath his fingertips. Guy could just imagine the sweet ache of it as he massaged her gently.

Dahlia felt her knees beginning to quiver, and she dropped her forehead to his shoulder and leaned against him for support. Guy rubbed a little harder and a little faster as she began to moan into his ear. He lifted her leg, raising it to the ledge of the shower, opening her widely for better access. He slid two fingers against her slit and slid them inside of her. Dahlia groaned at the sudden pressure and she tilted her hips toward him. Pulling his fingers out slowly, he pushed them back in. As he picked up his pace, Dahlia matched his rhythm, her hips bucking forward and backward against his hand.

Turning her around, Guy leaned her against the shower wall and kissed his way down her neck, stopping to take her dark nipples into his mouth. Water cascaded down over his neck and back, running into his mouth as he locked around her nipple. Dahlia's moans echoed off the bathroom tiles.

Lifting her leg back to the ledge he kissed his way down to her belly, pausing to dip his tongue into the curve of her belly button. His fingers danced back over her sweet spot, the folds open and wanting his attention. His fingers dipped back inside of her, and the whimper that passed between her lips had him steel-hard. He could feel his desire beginning to ooze as he spun her around to face the wall, her bottom pressing against his groin.

With one swift gesture, Guy entered her from behind. His loving was urgent and necessary, and with each thrust he could feel her muscles tightening like a vice around him, desperate to pull him in deeper. She sang his name over and over again until her voice grew strained and her legs quivered uncontrollably. With a fevered pitch he slammed himself in and out of her until neither of them could hold on a second longer. When every muscle from her abdomen to her thighs contracted in ecstasy, Guy's own release flooded from his body, and the intensity of the orgasm shook them both.

Guy held on to her until her last waves of rapture washed over them both. Dahlia slowly opened her eyes, beginning to catch her breath. Spinning back around in Guy's arms, she hugged him tightly, losing herself in his dark eyes as he stood staring at her. Having been in the shower for so long, the water had lost most of its heat. Guy reached around to turn the flow off, and the last drops echoed on the shower floor. Without saying a word, Dahlia cupped his face between her palms and kissed him effortlessly. Her kiss promised him forever, the passion as intense as the first time their two lips had touched.

"I love you, Guy Boudreaux," she said quietly, her sweet smile searing his heart.

"I love you more, Dahlia Morrow!" he echoed, brushing his thumb softly across her lower lip.

Stepping out of the shower, Dahlia reached for a large towel that rested on the bathroom counter. She wrapped it around his shoulders, patting his skin gently. Everything around them was covered with condensation, the mirrors steamed over and the wallpaper moist.

Dahlia laughed. "We have been in here way too long," she said softly. "We're going to be late if we don't get a move on it."

"Late is good. It means we're going to make an entrance," Guy responded.

Moving into the bedroom, Guy kissed her all the way to the bed, her girlish giggles prompting him to smile. When the backs of her knees leaned against the bed, he contemplated throwing her against the mattress and sinking himself inside her. He settled for drying her off, kissing her all over as he did. Dahlia returned the favor, pausing as she flicked her tongue against the ticklish spot that made him laugh.

"You really need to stop," he chided. "We need to get dressed." He leaned to kiss her one last time, then spun her around, slapped her bare bottom and gently pushed her in the direction of her walk-in closet.

Dahlia groaned, the low throbbing between her legs enough to make her want to forget about where they needed to be headed. As she watched him reach for the black tuxedo hanging from the closet door, she smiled, joy spreading like fire across her heart. They were just going to have to be late, she concluded as she admired his naked backside. She moved behind him and slapped his butt playfully.

As Guy turned around to scold her, Dahlia cupped her breasts in the palms of her hands and squeezed the lush tissue, tempting him. Her nipples had hardened in the room's cool air, and desire coursed through her veins. Their gazes met and held—the moment was electrifying. Guy's stomach lurched with an intensity that couldn't be explained, and he devoured her with a lust-filled look before tossing his tuxedo to the carpeted floor.

He followed as she moved backward toward the bed, her gaze still locked with his, her hands still teasing and taunting her breasts and nipples. As she reached the bed, he moved against her, the space between them growing heated. He leaned to kiss her, nibbling her lips as his hands traveled down her body, his hands clasping her bottom as he pulled her tightly to him.

Guy suddenly felt like everything had come into sharp focus, his entire body wakening from a long sleep. The sheer delight of Dahlia's touch, her mouth teasing sensations through the pit of his stomach had him lost in the sheer pleasure that ignited every one of his nerve endings.

Falling across the mattress, they sank into an endless dance of lips against lips. Dropping his weight against her, he delighted in how she parted her thighs and hooked her legs behind his back. A low groan escaped his mouth as Dahlia reached between them for his rising erection. He sighed into her mouth and breathed her name, whispering his love against her lips.

Slow and methodical with his loving, Guy eased himself inside of her. He teased and taunted her femininity until every muscle in her body melted into bliss. Her whole being shuddered as she began to spasm, the waves of her orgasm igniting his own. Guy shook and shuddered against her, crying out in long moans as they rode the waves of an intense orgasm. With an insatiable thirst, he couldn't get enough of her, and he loved her again and again.

Hours later as she lay in the crook of his arm they held each other for some time, taking in the magnitude of the moment. Dahlia took in the sounds of the stereo playing softly in the adjacent bathroom as Guy made jokes that moved her to laughter.

Outside the sun had begun to set and a black limousine sat patiently in the driveway.

* * *

On Hollywood Boulevard high-intensity searchlights crisscrossed the night sky as a crowd gathered in front of Grauman's Chinese Theatre. Movie stars were arriving in stretch limos to the applause of an adoring crowd. On the red carpet TV reports interviewed the who's who of movie stardom while photographers shot photos of the celebrities walking the red carpet. It was a quintessential Hollywood experience and neither Guy nor Dahlia cared that they were going to be late for the premiere of *Passionate*.

"Dahlia! Guy!"
"Here, Dahlia!"
"Guy, smile!"
Dahlia Morrow Boudreaux could not have been happier as she stepped out of the limousine in front of the Kodak Theatre on Hollywood Boulevard for the Eighty-Eighth Academy Awards. The paparazzi were desperate for her attention as cameras flashed around her, complete strangers screaming her name.

"We love you, Dahlia!"
The only other celebrity receiving more attention than her was Guy Boudreaux; the man looked like a million bucks in his Christian Dior silk tuxedo. The crowd was screaming his name as loudly.

"Guy! Over here, Guy! We love you, Guy!"
At the start of the red carpet the couple posed together, Guy's arm wrapped gently around Dahlia's waist, his large hand perched against the swell of her pregnant belly. They were both smiling sweetly as their

gazes skated over the landscape of actors and film critics, photographers and television hosts who had turned
out to celebrate their successes. The attention lavished
on the two of them was astounding; both were overwhelmed by the public fascination with their love story.

It had taken more than hard work to get her and Guy
to this moment, and as Dahlia paused in reflection and
her own hand gently caressed the swell of new life that
warmed her spirit, she was overcome with joy, savoring the beauty of it all.

As they continued their slow stroll down the red carpet, pausing for snapshots and interviews, they stopped
to acknowledge the other stars of the evening, Best
Actress nominee Zahara and her new husband, Owen
Kestner. The two couples posed for pictures, and Zahara congratulated them both on their pregnancy.

"Owen and I are thinking about adopting a baby
from overseas," she whispered into Dahlia's ear.

Dahlia smiled, her eyes wide with wonder as the
two moved ahead of them. An eager reporter pulled at
Guy's attention, curious to know how they would celebrate if he won the Oscar for Best Actor.

Guy paused, his brilliant smile washing over her.
"Tonight isn't about me," he said, his tone thought-
ful and reflective. "This is Dahlia's night. *Passionate*
has been a challenge from start to finish, and my part
pales in comparison to all that she did to bring this
film to life."

Dahlia smiled as Guy took her hand, lifting it to his
lips to kiss the backs of her fingers. Cameras flashed
furiously around them. As they made their way in-

side, Dahlia couldn't have been happier. Nothing could have made that moment more perfect, she thought as she walked the red carpet with the man she was head over heels in love with, evidence of their love growing inside of her.

Absolutely nothing at all.

* * * * *

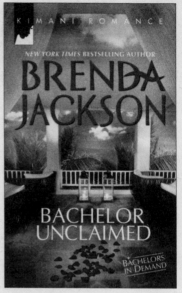

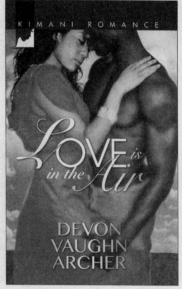

REQUEST YOUR FREE BOOKS!

2 FREE NOVELS
PLUS 2 FREE GIFTS!

KIMANI™
ROMANCE

Love's ultimate destination!

YES! Please send me 2 FREE Kimani™ Romance novels and my 2 FREE gifts (gifts are worth about $10). After receiving them, if I don't wish to receive any more books, I can return the shipping statement marked "cancel." If I don't cancel, I will receive 4 brand-new novels every month and be billed just $4.94 per book in the U.S. or $5.49 per book in Canada. That's a savings of at least 21% off the cover price. It's quite a bargain! Shipping and handling is just 50¢ per book in the U.S. and 75¢ per book in Canada.* I understand that accepting the 2 free books and gifts places me under no obligation to buy anything. I can always return a shipment and cancel at any time. Even if I never buy another book, the two free books and gifts are mine to keep forever.

168/368 XDN FVUK

Name	(PLEASE PRINT)	
Address		Apt. #
City	State/Prov.	Zip/Postal Code

Signature (if under 18, a parent or guardian must sign)

Mail to the **Harlequin® Reader Service:**
IN U.S.A.: P.O. Box 1867, Buffalo, NY 14240-1867
IN CANADA: P.O. Box 609, Fort Erie, Ontario L2A 5X3

Want to try two free books from another line?
Call 1-800-873-8635 or visit www.ReaderService.com.

* Terms and prices subject to change without notice. Prices do not include applicable taxes. Sales tax applicable in N.Y. Canadian residents will be charged applicable taxes. Offer not valid in Quebec. This offer is limited to one order per household. Not valid for current subscribers to Kimani Romance books. All orders subject to credit approval. Credit or debit balances in a customer's account(s) may be offset by any other outstanding balance owed by or to the customer. Please allow 4 to 6 weeks for delivery. Offer available while quantities last.

Your Privacy—The Harlequin® Reader Service is committed to protecting your privacy. Our Privacy Policy is available online at www.ReaderService.com or upon request from the Harlequin Reader Service.

We make a portion of our mailing list available to reputable third parties that offer products we believe may interest you. If you prefer that we not exchange your name with third parties, or if you wish to clarify or modify your communication preferences, please visit us at www.ReaderService.com/consumerchoice or write to us at Harlequin Reader Service Preference Service, P.O. Box 9062, Buffalo, NY 14269. Include your complete name and address.

KROM13

The right love can build you up....

Farrah Rochon

ALWAYS *And* FOREVER

Before Phylicia Philips can buy her cherished home back, architect Jamal Johnson beats her to the punch. He plans to completely renovate the old place—and wants Phylicia to help him! And though she doesn't trust Jamal, she's helpless to fight the passion simmering between them. Will they be able to build a blueprint for love?

∽ BAYOU DREAMS ∾